The Delegate

Edward Mwangi

Moran (E.A.) Publishers Limited,
Judda Complex, Prof. Wangari Maathai Road,
P.O. Box 30797-00100, Nairobi, Kenya

With offices and representatives in: Uganda, Rwanda, Tanzania, Malawi and
Zambia

www.moranpublishers.com

First Published, 2012.

ISBN 978 9966 34 534 9
ebook - ISBN 978 9966 63 221 0

2022   2021   2020   2019   2018
22   21   20   19   18   17   16   15   14   13

FOREWORD

The National Book Development Council of Kenya (NBDCK) is a Kenyan nongovernmental organization made up of stakeholders from the book and education sectors. It is mandated to promote the love of reading, the importance of books and quality education.

In November 2010, the NBDCK partnered with the Canadian Organization for Development through Education (CODE) to introduce in Kenya the Burt Award for African Literature, which involves identification, development and distribution of quality story books targeting the youth, and awarding the author. The purpose for the Burt Award books such as The Delegate is to avail to the reader high quality, engaging and enjoyable books whose content is portrayed in an environment the reader can easily identify with thereby arousing his/her interest to read and to continue reading. This sharpens the reader's English language and comprehension skills leading to a better understanding of the other subjects.

The NBDCK would like to thank Bill Burt for sponsoring and allowing the Burt Award for African Literature to be introduced in Kenya. Special thanks also go to the panel of judges for their professional input into this project. Finally, this foreword would be incomplete without recognizing the important role played by all the NBDCK stakeholders whose continued support and involvement in the running of NBDCK has ensured the success of the first Burt Award in Kenya.

Ruth K. Odondi
Chief Executive Officer
National Book Development Council of Kenya

ACKNOWLEDGEMENT

The Burt Award for African Literature recognizes excellence in young adult fiction from African countries. It supports the writing and publication of high quality, culturally relevant books and ensures their distribution to schools and libraries to help develop young people's literacy skills and foster their love of reading. The Burt Award is generously sponsored by a Canadian philanthropist, Bill Burt, and is part of the ongoing literacy programmes of the National Book Development Council of Kenya, and CODE, a Canadian NGO supporting development through education for over 50 years.

Chapter One

Everything pointed to the coming of a heavy downpour that Monday afternoon. Dark clouds from the eastern horizon that moved fast due to a strong, blustery wind, were rapidly forming in the sky. The wind blew dry leaves and dust all over the compound forcing pupils of Kipyego Primary School to cut short their afternoon break. They rushed to their classrooms with many pupils rejoicing at the sudden change in the weather. It had been four months since it rained. Intense famine had struck the area killing livestock and leaving many families without a source of income. The community living around Marigat relied heavily on livestock for survival. A number of people had also succumbed to hunger; the monthly government food donation was inadequate. It could only feed a family for two days.

Milcah Chebet was quiet at her desk, flipping the pages of the English textbook she had placed on the rough surface. As far as she was concerned, the rain was four months too late. Had it come earlier, she thought, she would not have lost her beloved grandmother to famine three weeks back. She was there when her grandmother died and she sobbed helplessly. None of her family members could give her grandmother food.

Chebet was the first born in a family of three. After her father was killed in the violence that followed a disputed presidential election in 2007, her mother assumed the role of the breadwinner until a month ago when she was diagnosed with what the doctors called severe colon cancer. Life got worse for Chebet and her siblings who had to rely on the school feeding programme run by the Kenya Red Cross. Their mother, too, survived gracefully through the programme. Chebet and her siblings hid some food which they took home to their bedridden mother every day except Saturday and Sunday when they did not go to school. It was too little but enough to keep her alive.

As usual, Chebet had hidden the food in her old and torn school bag and was waiting for the end of the school day to take the food home to her mother and her younger brother. They took turns to look after their mother. Today was her brother's turn.

She stared blankly at her classmates as they danced in class, rejoicing that the rain had come. Their bare feet blew dust into the air.

"Cheb, why do you study so hard yet your mother can't afford to take you to a secondary school?" Kipchirchir mocked her, pushing the English book aside.

Chebet looked intently at him, dying to respond, but for the chuckling and sneering by some girls which prevented her. She blinked repeatedly in a bid to stop tears from trickling down her cheeks.

"Have you carried food for your mother?" Kipchirchir continued to mock her.

He tried to grab her bag but Chebet held it firmly. She could not hold back the tears anymore.

"Leave me alone," she cried as other pupils gathered around them to watch the unfolding drama. Kipchirchir could not let go of his hold on the bag resulting in a tug of war, much to the delight of their classmates who cheered them on.

"Leave her alone. Stop it!" Janet, Chebet's close friend, shouted from the open door. She rushed to the desk and pushed Kipchirchir away. He loosened his grip and fell on the floor, releasing Chebet's bag. Their classmates cheered on oblivious of the gathering storm.

A furious Chebet walked out of the class with her bag. She almost collided with a boy who was running across the verandah. She started walking hurriedly.

"Young girl, where are you going?" she felt a hand on her shoulders and recognised her head teacher's deep, commanding voice. She was lost for words.

"Are you running away from school?" the head teacher asked.

Chebet turned and faced him. She did not know what to say.

"You have been a very bright girl but you are now performing poorly because of this kind of behaviour. Is it because you have started growing breasts, eeh? You think you are the first girl to become a woman, eeh? I am talking to you!" he said as he shook her by the shoulders.

She looked at him with intense pain and tears continued to flow from her eyes.

"I'm not interested in your tears and mucus. Kneel down!" he ordered her.

Chebet stared at him in disbelief.

God, why is this happening? Who will ever understand me? Chebet wondered silently.

He slapped her across the face when she hesitated to kneel down. A whirl of dust then covered them both forcing Mr Muchoki, as he was called, to face the other direction. Chebet thought of taking off but just then she saw her brother running towards them. She wondered why he had left their mother on her own but before she could ask him, the head teacher interrupted.

"Are you Julius?" he asked callously.

"Yes, I'm..."

"Nonsense!" he roared. "What are you doing here without school uniform?"

"He was..."

"Shut up!" he shouted just as Chebet tried to explain. "Both of you go to my office and kneel down in front of my desk. I'm sending someone to call your sick mother to explain. Off to my office. Fast!" he ordered.

Chebet rose and started to walk towards the office. Her brother walked by her side. Mr Muchoki remained behind.

"Mum wants to see you, Cheb. She is very sick. Have you carried our food?" he asked softly.

"What is wrong with her? Why did you leave her alone?" she asked, as they walked towards the office, the head teacher now steps behind them. He stopped to speak to a pupil and fell farther behind.

A day that was sweltering hot at noon was now covered with dark clouds. Rain had started to fall. The moistened soil had a nice smell to it.

"We have to go home Cheb," he said, sorrow overwhelming him. "I have never seen mother look as bad as she does today."

"But we have to go to the head teacher's office," Cheb responded.

"We shall be caned, let's run home. Mum wants to see you immediately. She said that she wants to speak with you. She is speaking so weakly, Cheb."

Chebet stopped walking a few metres away from the head teacher's office. She looked at her brother.

"She is also very hungry Cheb. Remember she did not eat yesterday. She can't move any of her limbs. I saw some pus too. She was crying, Cheb."

"What?"

He looked away. She noticed the sadness in him. His eyes became watery. He was shaking his head despondently. His dark round face appeared much darker. For the first time she noticed that her brother had grown thinner. His eyes were sparkling white while his skin had turned rough and scaly. She could not control herself and broke into tears.

"Is there such a thing as good life?" She asked herself silently. "Are there people with so much food that they throw some away?"

She looked back and saw the head teacher approaching them. He now had a cane in one hand; with the other, he was dragging a pupil along. The rain was more intense now.

"Let's go, Julius," she started to run.

The head teacher shouted for her to stop but she ignored him. She did not look back. She could hear her brother run behind her. She held the bag firmly to herself and continued running.

Chapter Two

The blustery wind continued to wreak havoc, blowing in all directions. There were no signs that the heavy rain would stop soon as the whole sky was covered with dark nimbus clouds. Chebet and her brother were drenched to the skin. Her bag was dripping with water. Her books were soaked.

"Cheb, let's shelter from the rain at the shop," Julius implored her while pointing at one of the tin shacks that served as shops at the shopping centre. A number of people were standing by the verandah of the three shops sheltering themselves from the rain. Chebet knew it was risky to walk in the rain as they could be struck by lightning, which was a common occurrence in Marigat. Anytime it happened, people blamed it on witchcraft.

"If we stop, we may not cross the river as it is likely to break its banks," Chebet responded while splashing the water that had formed in paddles on the ground with her feet. She was right, for water from the hills flowed into the river with so much force that it swept away everything in its path. What is more, one could easily drown in the swollen river. Her sick mother wanted to see her. No amount of rain would stop her from getting home to her mother.

"Do you think the head teacher will chase us away from school for defying him and running away?" Chebet finally asked, wiping her face with the back of her hand. Julius did not respond.

"Maybe he will chase me away from the school," she finally commented, shifting the old and torn school bag to her left hand. Her equally old and torn green school pullover stuck to her patched green dress. Her mother had mended it several times for they could not afford new school uniforms. They did not worry about shoes; their bare feet would serve just as well.

"What will happen if the head teacher chases us away? Where shall we get our food?"

All was silent apart from the sound of their feet in the running water and the falling rain.

"Chebet, do you think life would be this desperate if father were alive?" Julius asked while trying to catch up with his sister who was walking fast.

"Life was good when he was alive. I miss him," Chebet commented.

"Why did they kill him? Did he steal from anyone?"

"No."

Lightning struck from the east followed by deafening thunder, drowning what Chebet wanted to say. It scared Julius so much that he grabbed onto his sister's dress. A goat that had stopped on the road ran off in shock, splashing water on both of them. Julius moved to the right of Chebet.

Chebet started to jog once again, her pullover dripping with water. Julius, his hold on her dress still firm, struggled to match her pace. There were no other people on the rough road, only goats and cattle that stood still, not minding the heavy rain. Maybe they were happy that it had rained and grass would grow.

Julius's grip on Chebet's dress loosened sending him sprawling to the soggy ground.

"I'm sorry," Chebet said as she helped her brother up from the ground. He started crying, holding the big toe of his right leg, which was bleeding into the rainwater.

"Please stand. We cannot stop."

"It's painful, Chebet."

"I know, but mother is alone. No one is there to take care of her. I know she is being rained on. Let's hurry home to her."

"My leg is… I can't move!" Julius wailed, sitting down in the running water. Chebet was getting impatient and with arms akimbo, threatened: "Get up or I will leave you here!"

Her brother continued crying, his tears making an insignificant contribution to the flowing rainwater.

Chebet walked away and did not stop when her brother started wailing.

"Mother is being rained on and she hasn't eaten since Saturday. She cannot move in case the house is leaking right where she is lying in bed," Chebet told herself and walked even faster.

At this thought, she started running, the school bag still in her hands. She persisted with the running even when her body called for some rest. She was home in thirty minutes. The door to their small house was open. The wind had blown off part of the thatched roof letting in the rain and leaving the wooden seats, clothes and utensils soaked. She pulled aside the polyester material that separated her mother's bedroom from the kitchen.

The kitchen was what one noticed when they entered the small grass-thatched house. Chebet's house did not have a sitting room. Any time they wanted to rest in the house, they did that in the room that served as the kitchen, dining and sitting rooms. A mud wall with numerous cracks and two polyester cloths that served as doors separated the main room from the bedrooms.

She hastily entered her mother's bedroom. Her heart raced as she studied the room. She gazed at the roof and tears flowed freely from her eyes.

"Mother, I'm sorry."

Her mother lay motionless on the bed. She was drenched for she could not move away from the rain falling on her sickly and emaciated body. She was not covered with anything and the checked, torn dress she wore stuck to her body. Chebet noticed her mother was shaking.

"Mother, I'm sorry," she apologised again as she moved towards her mother who faced the muddy wall and was too weak to even turn around and look at her. At her touch, Chebet's mother responded by opening her eyes weakly. Chebet noticed the sadness on her mother's face and was dumbfounded when she noticed tears flowing down her mother's face. She was crying quietly. Chebet did not know how to respond. She gave her mother a long despondent look. Her body had shrunk.

Her mother extended her hand, which Chebet held. It was dark, thin and very cold. She forgot about the rain falling on both of them. She smiled back when she noticed the weak smile on her mother's face.

"Here is your food mother, Mother" Chebet said, removing the food from her bag. Her mother shook her head perhaps to decline.

"Mother, you haven't eaten since Saturday. You are so weak and thin. Please eat."

"Tha-nk y-o-u so…" she muttered weakly, more tears flowing from her eyes and trickling down to the bed. She gasped in pain.

Chebet could not control her tears. A strong wind followed, blowing away more of the thatch from the roof.

"Where shall we go if this rain continues? What will I do? No, I will repair the roof by putting back the thatch," she said aloud.

Her mother gestured to her.

Chebet knelt on the mushy ground. Her mother tried to move her hand but was unable.

"Cheb-et thank-you-for what-you ha-ve done," she paused, wincing in pain. Her eyes were white. She looked like someone who did not have any blood.

"Take ca-re of your bro-thers," she said and closed her eyes. Chebet waited.

"You wi-ll qu-it s-ch-ool and get marri-ed. Talk to yo-ur-uncle Nor-be-rt. He wi-ll org-an-i-se for that and your ini-ti-a-tion. Take ca-re of…"

"Mother, no! I want to finish school and…"

"Cheb, No o-ne wi-ll take care of th-em," she muttered. "Only yo-u," she stopped talking but Chebet noticed that her lips were moving. She bent down further to listen to her but the muttering stopped. Her body started to quiver. Chebet held her firmly on the bed.

"Mother!" she called out with dread.

Her body shook again then stopped.

"Mother! Please talk to me," she started wailing. Her mother was not responding and her body seemed relaxed. Her mouth was half open while her eyes remained closed.

"Mother!" Chebet screamed.

Julius entered the house wailing. He was limping and dripping wet. Chebet ignored him and continued screaming. She was shaking her mother gently wondering why she was not responding.

Her mother lay motionless on the bed, her hands outstretched.

"No, she cannot die like my grandmother," Chebet said to no one in particular.

She wailed uncontrollably, frightening Julius.

"I told you she was hungry. Give her the food Cheb," he told her.

Chebet continued wailing.

Chapter Three

Chebet leant gently on one of the tent posts. Her eight-year old brother stood by her side, sucking on his thumb oblivious to what was happening. He gazed curiously at the wooden coffin that held the remains of their mother. Chebet wondered whether her brother understood that once one died, they never came back; they stayed dead. This is what was tormenting her. It had been on her mind for ten days since her mother died. Her mother had followed her father so soon. They were now orphans. She had no doubt that their life was to become wretched and that she would never achieve her cherished dream.

"When the night is so dark, when the night is so long, never forget one thing: the sun will ultimately come and the darkness of the night will be gone," Chebet thought to herself.

She shook her head as she held the arm of her brother and led him to an empty seat at the back of the tent. She did not like the pitiful look on the faces of the people who had attended the burial of her mother. They all looked so concerned, including the relatives who came in large numbers and acted generous at the home. She knew that they were all pretending; she could not rely on any of them for assistance. Though most of her relatives were poor, the well-off among them had promised to assist them when they lost their father. After their father's burial, everything came to an end and none came to check on them. When their mother fell sick none came to see her let alone take her to hospital. She was left to the care of her children. Chebet was convinced that the same promises would be given. Her life and that of her siblings were doomed, she thought. The words of the teacher she loved at her school could not work. The sun will never shine and the morning will never dawn.

"Excuse me, Chebet," her aunt startled her back to reality, "The pastor is asking for you and your brothers. Please come to the house."

Chebet rose lazily from the seat and walked with her brother to the house. Her youngest brother, Dennis, stood at the door to the house, dressed in old denim shorts. Sadness overwhelmed Chebet as she entered the house. Memories of her last days with her mother came flooding back. She fought back tears as she shook hands with the pastor.

"Chebet, we are sorry for what happened to your family," the pastor started speaking in his hoarse voice. A couple of relatives stood by the pastor, including the uncle whom her mother had mentioned before she died. He was aging with grey hair all over his head. He was the elder brother of her father and was the only relative who had visited them, though only occasionally. Chebet did not like his rough manners, and she hated his first wife who had not even attended the burial – the woman was not on talking terms with Chebet's mother. Chebet reciprocated by not talking to them either. The uncle's second wife was young but good to Chebet and her siblings. She had a loose bladder and occasionally urinated on herself. For this reason, she kept to herself.

"We know the good work you did - cleaning your mother almost daily and ensuring that she had something to eat. God will bless you. We shall pray together and ask God to guide you, give you strength and make you grow up as good children. Please hold your brothers' hands as we pray."

She held Dennis with her right hand and Julius with the left. The pastor said a long prayer. Chebet walked out of the house right after the prayers and went behind the house, previously a cattle shed. There were no cattle since they all died due to the long dry spell.

"Who will now stay with us, Chebet?" Dennis asked when he got to the place where she was standing. Chebet looked askance at the clear sky and bit her lower lip.

"Cheb who will take care of us?"

"The school will. I will be there too," she answered still gazing at the sky.

She supported herself on one of the stumps that stood erect next to her. She felt dizzy.

"You will quit school and get married," she recalled her mother's words. She looked at the sky again and vehemently shook her head. Girls her age got married to old men who paid dowry – goats and cows – to their families. The number of livestock a family owned was a sign of its wealth. Marrying off one's daughters was a good way of increasing the number of cows and goats; that is why parents gladly married off their daughters from the age of twelve. Some of Chebet's friends got married at that age.

However, Chebet had to first get circumcised to be considered mature. She never thought much of these rituals for she was not planning to observe them. Her dream was to get educated and one day advocate the rights of marginalised girls and women. This was now going down the drain. She wondered whether she could evade all these traditions.

"Shall we continue with school? Mr Muchoki does not like us," Julius said, interrupting her thoughts.

"You are required at the tent. The funeral service is about to begin," a distant relative informed them.

They followed her and were directed to the front seats, close to the pastor who was leading the service. There were just a few people; not enough to require the pastor to use a loudspeaker. However, preaching loudly came naturally to the pastor, loudspeaker or none.

He started the service with a series of hymns that prepared the people for the sombre sermon ahead. Everyone kept on staring at the bereaved children. Chebet noticed Miriam, her mother's friend, sobbing while looking at them.

"We are gathered here once again to celebrate the gift of life and to thank God for resting our beloved sister, Monica Chelimo. We were here a few months ago when we gathered to send off our dear father. God has visited this home once again and has rested the soul of our dear sister who is now at peace at the right hand of the Father," he swallowed some saliva loudly. "We cannot condemn God for doing this but we appreciate His favour," the pastor continued.

Chebet's thoughts drifted to the spate of misfortunes that had struck her family. She wondered why God had sent the angel of darkness to their home so frequently.

I wish he never visited us. Who will take care of us now? How will our life be? Will any of these relatives take us to their home? No, they will do just like they did after my father died. They will promise good things, but will all leave after the burial. Do I get married? What about my dreams? Why does God choose death for some people? Chebet wondered silently.

Tears streamed down Chebet's cheeks as she gazed blankly at the coffin that carried her mother's body. She held her younger brother's hand and tried to concentrate on the pastor's preaching.

"Chebet, you are the first born in this family," the pastor said as he faced her. Everyone gave them a sad, worried look. "Please take care of your brothers. Do not forget them or abandon them, even if you get married. I know you are still young but stand firm in life and God will not let you down. This is not the end of life, but rather, the beginning of some good things that will happen to this family. God will stand by you," he continued.

Chebet did not see how life would turn out joyful.

Numerous people spoke, as usual, promising good things. Many spoke emotionally and sentimentally, giving an account of their relationship with her mother. Chebet knew they were lying for they hardly visited them when her mother was sick. She felt sick of everyone, including the last speaker.

"I am a friend of this home. I spoke several times with the mother. I visited her and we talked a lot. I am a friend of Chebet's uncle and I am promising to assist each one of these children."

Chebet sneered unconsciously as she listened to the man whom she later learnt was meant to be her future husband. Bitterness and wrath boiled inside her while her stomach rumbled loudly and her legs trembled. She was glad when he finished. She followed him with her eyes as he walked to where her uncle, Norbert, sat.

"We will now escort the body of our sister to her final resting place," the pastor said before asking a few people to carry the coffin.

Chebet struggled to breathe while her heart thumped harder. One of her aunts held her arm and led her to the graveside. Chebet gazed at an empty space incredulously as the pastor prayed for her mother's soul.

"You were not supposed to bring the children to the graveside. Take them back!" the pastor addressed her aunt who tried to move her away but she resisted.

"It's okay. The mistake cannot be undone," the pastor remarked before embarking on the final ritual.

"I will never see you, Mum. You are gone forever and left us without parents. It started with Father. Now it's you. Why this? Why? Who is left with us? Why, Mother?" Chebet asked herself.

The world around her started to spin. A cold sweat ran down her spine and she felt hammers bang ceaselessly in her brains.

"Why did you have to die, Mother? No, this is not true. Why did you accept to die, Mother?" Chebet asked herself again.

Her vision started to blur. She could swear her heartbeats were audible and she felt adrenaline pour into her stomach, literally. She was sweating profusely.

"Mother!" she shrieked.

She stretched her arm for support when she realised she, too, was spinning. She fell on her mother's coffin and everything around her slipped into darkness.

Chapter Four

She rose and sat on the edge of the bed. She massaged her forehead with the right hand to ease the splitting headache. She supported herself with her left hand and continued to relive what had happened the previous day. She could not recall what had happened as soon as they got to the graveside. She had collapsed and only regained her consciousness two hours later. By then, the burial service was over and a number of people had already left her home. When she regained her energy, her aunt, under the instructions of her uncle, took Chebet and her siblings to her home, almost three kilometres away. Chebet did not want to leave her home. Indeed, she could not imagine leaving her home. She felt like she was leaving her mother alone. She wanted to stay behind and keep her mother company.

She heard a knock at the door. She rose indolently from the bed and approached the door. Her body was very weak and her head ached terribly. She had not eaten since the day before but she was not hungry at all.

"Chebet, today is Monday. Are we going to school?" her brother, Dennis, asked.

Chebet remained quiet. She was not sure she would ever go back to school. She had dreamt big while at school, assuring herself that she would go all the way to the university and set an example in her village where children only knew about rearing cattle and early marriages. However, this dream seemed to have hit a snag; she was likely to terminate her education. She needed a source of income to support her siblings. She did not know how she could do it but she knew she had to.

"They did not carry our school uniform along. I want to go to school, Aunt" Dennis complained, tears in his eyes. Chebet stared blankly at the sparsely furnished sitting room.

"We cannot go to school today," she finally responded, her heart heavy with sadness and grief.

"When?"

"I don't know, Dennis."

Her aunt walked in with a jug half-filled with milk.

"You have woken up very early, Chebet. You know you can't go to school now."

"I want to go to school, aunt," Dennis said and started to cry.

Chebet felt irritated by her brother and quietly walked out of the house. She moved towards a log at the end of the house and sat on it. Her brother followed, tears streaming down his eyes. Chebet had cried so much that her eyes had become swollen and itchy.

As she gazed at the fast rising sun, she recalled the words of Mr Mwenda, her favourite teacher. "Chebet, you are a very strong girl. You are very intelligent and mature. A great future awaits you. Stand strong and never sit on your potential."

Mr Mwenda had been transferred to another school three months earlier. She wished she could see him and tell him the new development in her life. At one time the words seemed very real. She could see herself as a successful woman. Now the words appeared illusory and Chebet was convinced that her future would not be as she had thought.

"How are you, Chebet?" Uncle Norbert greeted her. "Are you alright?"

She looked at her brother who was sitting on the ground staring at the sky. He was not fine. His face was full of sadness. Chebet, too, was not fine.

"I'm fine, Uncle," she responded.

Silence descended between them.

"Julius and Dennis would like to go to school."

"What about you?" he asked.

"No."

"Why? Where do you want to go?" he asked with concern in his voice.

"I will go to the quarry and find work. That way, I will get some money and look after my siblings," she answered resolutely. "Other children are doing the same and helping their families."

"But only boys and men go to the quarry."

"My mother used to before she fell sick. She used to get us food."

"Chebet, that is unacceptable. I will not allow it. You will not go to the quarry."

"Who will provide for us if I don't work? My grandmother could not work. She died of hunger. No one brought her food. My mother fell sick and had to rely on the school feeding programme. Where shall we get our food if we or I do not work?" she asked boldly, her mouth trembling.

"You will not go there."

Chebet had never imagined working at the quarry. She had dreamt of getting a well-paying job which could earn her money to take care of her family. She had hoped to one day assist her villagemates and ensure that they were recognised countrywide. She had not been to many other places but her teachers said that their village was far behind in its development – living in a house with electricity was unimaginable while having water flow from taps sounded miraculous.

Her brother emerged from the house. He stretched and yawned as though very hungry, exposing his bony ribs before walking towards Chebet and Julius.

"Are we going home?" he asked, ignoring his uncle who stood a few metres from Chebet.

"Dennis, do you want to go home?" the uncle asked wryly.

"Yes. This is not our home. Is it, Chebet?"

She shook her head.

"Chebet," her uncle looked at her quizzically. "You said you want to work in the quarry so that you can support your siblings? Will that be enough?"

"It is the best option, Uncle. We have survived through the school food. What I will get at the quarry will be sufficient. As it is, no one needs a housegirl in this area."

"But they may need someone to look after their cattle. I can do that, Chebet. They will then pay me and then we can buy food, right?" Dennis interrupted. Chebet looked at him with pity.

"You will go back to school."

"But I know the head teacher will refuse to take us back."

"He will let you return. He knows what happened." Chebet responded courageously. "We cannot all quit school, Dennis."

Their uncle shook his head and looked away. Maybe he was watching the herd of cattle that had left for pasture. One of Chebet's cousins had the task of looking after the cattle. He did not go to school but was very comfortable looking after cattle. It was like a profession. Boys who did this task were loved in the family and treated like kings. Due to the famine that had struck the area, the boys were allowed to drink milk straight from the cows.

"You cannot all quit," their uncle responded.

There was silence as their aunt approached with a kettle in her hands. She served each of them tea without sugar. Dennis almost knocked the cup over as he greedily grabbed it to sip the hot tea. He was not used to taking tea. They rarely took breakfast; when they did, it was porridge. Some months back, they used to take milk but all that stopped when their cows and goats died.

"You will scald yourself with tea," Julius warned.

"Is it too hot, Julius?" her aunt asked with care.

He took a jug and started cooling the tea. Chebet was too deep in thought to notice that her tea was getting cold. She did not notice when her aunt approached with a seat. She sat down and slowly started to take her tea.

"We need to go to the chief's camp. The relief food will be supplied today," her aunt said. "Each family will get ten kilogrammes of maize, five kilogrammes of beans, two kilogrammes of cooking fat and two kilogrammes of rice."

"But what will that do? How long can it last a family?" she asked indifferently.

Chebet knew that the food donation was not much. Indeed, by the time the government returned after three weeks or a month, a number of people would have died of hunger. It was never enough for them. The government had promised that no one else would die of hunger but several had died and continued to die. They died even when parts of the country had more than enough maize – so much so that it went bad. Potatoes and cabbages were rotting in some parts of the country.

"Who will take ours?" Dennis asked.

"We shall take the food for you. The chief knows about your case."

"But who will cook for us?" Julius asked.

"Chebet will do it," her aunt answered.

"Oh, before I forget, Dennis and Julius, call Onesmus here to take his tea before he takes the livestock out to graze."

"I have not finished my tea," Julius protested.

"Just go," the aunt responded, "Your tea will be here when you return."

He rose angrily and followed Dennis.

"Chebet," her uncle started as soon as her brothers had left, "Your mother must have talked to you, didn't she?"

"No, we did not talk," Chebet lied. "We had talked a night before she died but there was nothing to discuss. She only said…" she paused. "We did not talk," she said.

"It would have been better if you had talked but it's okay," he cleared his throat and faced her.

"You know, life has to go on for all of you after the death of your mother."

Chebet gasped.

"Your idea to start working in the quarry is good, but the pay is not sufficient to sustain your family. I discussed this with your mother," he paused to sip his tea.

"You are now a grown-up girl and you know that only one thing remains: you have to undergo female initiation, that is, circumcision. We do not condone uncircumcised women in our community as they are cursed and will not get married to anyone. You will have to…."

"No!" Chebet interrupted sharply.

"Please, let me finish. We agreed on this with your mother and she was to talk to you about it. You do not have a choice, Chebet. Girls become women by undergoing this cut," he responded firmly, annoyance written all over his face.

Her aunt looked away with a pained look.

"Every girl must undergo this process," he continued, "We do not entertain uncircumcised girls. We have already made plans and the whole process will be take place next week on…."

"I will not!" Chebet vowed rising from her chair, "I said no… and…"

Her uncle was stunned.

"I have told you! We are not discussing it and this must be done," he recovered in time to respond furiously and loudly, "After you heal, we shall start the dowry negotiations. You will be married to Mr Kipyeno by the time you approach…"

"I have said no. I would rather die like my mother. No! I won't do any of those things. You better kill me," she started shouting while crying.

Her brothers came back running when they heard her crying.

"Kill me! I will not do that!"

"What is wrong, Cheb?" Julius asked while Dennis just broke into tears.

"We are going home," she told her brothers. "Let's go home. I wish mother had not died. Let's go home," she started walking away while crying.

"Are you doing this because we do not have parents? You have made my sister cry because…" Julius started weeping as he followed his sister, pain overwhelming him.

"How do you… Chebet! Chebet! I'm calling you!" her uncle shouted. "Come back here!"

She started to run.

Chapter Five

They sat beside the road under the shadow of a spiky cactus plant. Dennis and Julius sat next to Chebet. The sun was getting hotter and the sky becoming clearer. There were no signs it would rain soon. Rains had become a bad souvenir; anytime she thought of the rains, she recalled the death of her mother and how they had slept beside her for a whole night, not knowing what to do nor who to call. They had not minded the rain water that dripped on them for the better part of that fateful night. It was a bad experience which she wished she could forget for the rest of her life.

She watched impassively as a herd of cattle and goats walked sluggishly on the rocky path. Two women followed later carrying containers full of water. One of the ladies carried her son on top of the container that she carried on her back. The water must have been fetched from the community well, almost ten kilometres away. That well served so many people and one could wait for almost four hours before their turn to fetch water. By that time, one was lucky to get water as it dried up during the day. People went there very early to avoid long queues. Chebet had gone there to fetch water before her mother died. After the death of her mother, the women who attended the funeral meetings came with water which was used sparingly. It was a precious commodity.

"Chebet, will you stay with us now that mother is no longer there?" Julius asked after the women had gone some distance.

"I will stay with you and I will take care of you," she answered while patting his back. "I will ensure that you complete your studies and that you will buy…" she gazed at the dry plains, a distant look on her face.

"But who will pay fees?

"Don't worry. I will ensure that you go to that school. I will get a job and pay for you. I will do the same for Julius," she said confidently.

"You are in Class Six. Our teacher told us that you cannot get a job if you don't complete your education," Dennis argued.

"Our teacher said that God always listens to the prayers of children. We need to pray and…" Dennis continued.

"We do not go to church," Julius argued.

Chebet remained silent for a while.

"Even if we do not go to church, God will listen to our prayer. We can pray to Him now, can't we?" Chebet looked at the heavens. "Let's kneel down and pray. He will listen to us."

They all knelt on the rocky road and innocently closed their eyes.

"God, I pray for our father and mother. I pray for Julius and Dennis. I also pray for myself," she paused, "Please God, protect us from the devil and help us go to school. God, I do not want…"

"Why do you want to cry, Cheb?" Julius asked after opening his eyes.

"Let's walk home," she finally said, wiping tears with the back of her hand.

"What are we going to do at home? Our teacher told us that there are pupils who assist their parents to cultivate their shamba," Julius said.

"Those are the ones who have a shamba that can be tilled. They grow everything on the land. We cannot do that because ours is dry. If we plant they will all dry up. Our cows died," Chebet responded bluntly as she stood to remove some dust from her old dress.

"We have nothing to do at our home," Julius reiterated.

"No, we have," she answered, "You shall go to school and leave me behind."

"What will you do?" Dennis asked.

"Let's go home. You shall go to school and when you come in the evening, I will tell you what we shall do. You have to complete your education. Dad expected us to do so," Chebet asserted.

The journey to their home took one hour. They were in their compound at noon.

"It's late, Cheb. Mr Muchoki will chase us away for being late," Julius argued.

"He knows that we were not in school because of our mother's burial."

"Cheb, you know last time we evaded his punishment," a worried Julius said. "I don't think he will let us in."

"He will, Julius. Please prepare yourself and put on the uniform. I will escort you."

"Chebet, are you coming with us?"

"Yes, but I will not be with you any more. Mother said that you should continue with school. When you finish, then I will continue with my education, no matter how old I will be," she told them.

"Didn't she say that you too should go back with us?" Dennis asked as he wore the tattered yellow shirt.

"I am the first born and have to take care of you. I can always go back to school when you finish," she answered.

She stood facing the small window that was covered with a hard carton paper. Her mother's words came flooding back into her mind.

She walked out of the house and looked at her mother's grave. It was just a day since her burial. The home that had a small crowd of people the day before was now empty of any life. Chebet fought back tears.

"I have to be strong," she resolved, "No one will take care of us but ourselves."

She went back to the house. Dennis was assisting Julius to force books into a torn polythene paper bag.

They both loved reading and Chebet knew they were excited about going back to school. She wished she could go with them. She had to support her brilliant brothers who always led their classes in exams. They all took after their father who was very intelligent. Had their deceased grandfather taken him for studies he would have become a very important person in society. Unfortunately, he could not afford school fees. Their father had no choice but to work in the quarry. However, he managed to take care of them, through the little he earned by hard work, resilience and determination. He ensured they had food and did not miss school.

"I will ensure that you get that which I did not get. It will be expensive, but I am determined to take you all the way to the university," he had once told them at supper time, months before he was killed. "Do not let me down when you grow up. I would like all of you to be good children; children who will come home and carry me in their cars. This will make me and your mother very proud."

Things were now different. Chebet doubted whether the dream of her father would come true.

"I will take your role, Father," she muttered.

"Please hurry, it's almost time. You need to be there by lunch time," she urged her brothers who walked out of the house hurriedly. They did not bathe and their feet showed as much; they were very dusty. There was nothing like oil to apply to their dry and rough skin.

Chebet accompanied them, walking fast while talking about everything and nothing. She felt bad that she could not go to school like her brothers. Though primary education was free, they required money for learning materials. They could not get the money if she chose to proceed with her education together with them. That is what her mother meant when she told her to take care of her siblings.

"I wish I were not a first born," she regretted silently.

"What will you go home to do?" Dennis asked her just before she turned back, a few metres from one of the many open school entrances. She remained quiet for a while.

She shook her head, a plastic smile playing on her lips, her face glowing in mock cheer.

"Please hurry up. It's almost lunch time; you may miss your lunch," she patted Dennis on the back. "I'm starting to work for you."

"I will bring you food, Cheb," Dennis said. Chebet looked back and gazed at her brother, an unexplained emotion tagging at her heart.

"For today, yes," she responded, "Tomorrow I will."

Dennis gave her an incredulous look.

"Chebet, you cannot go to work. You have not even completed Class Eight."

"Before mother died, she told me that I have to work and take care of you," she paused. "That begins now. Bye and see you in the evening."

She faced the other direction and started walking away, tears of despondency cascading down her cheeks. She missed school but she knew that she would not continue with it. She had to work first.

She looked back and saw her brothers disappear into the school. She sobbed softly as she walked sluggishly, wondering why life was unfair.

"Take care of your brothers," her mother had told her. She recalled those words as she walked feebly on the rocky and dusty road.

She did not enter her home when she got there. Instead, she walked past, determined to start the new life. She ignored an old woman who called her by name when she neared the home.

She had to face the wrath of being a first born.

Chapter Six

She sat quietly on a huge, shapeless rock immersed in deep thought, hardly blinking, but breathing hard. She crossed her legs and held her head between her hands. It was lunch time but she did not have food. All the same, she did not have the urge to eat anything. She was sure that she had grown thinner. Her classmates had nicknamed her, "The Sudanese," because of her dark complexion. She had taken after her father, a very dark man.

"If you want to succeed as a girl, you have to fight the early marriages in our area. You have to say no. You have to say no to female genital mutilation. Girls who want to succeed shun these practices. They concentrate on education," she nodded imperceptibly as she recalled the message of one celebrated woman, from Marigat Division, who was now a musician.

The woman had visited the school on several occasions and talked to Class Six, Seven and Eight girls. Chebet had listened carefully and taken the musician as a good model. She had vowed then that she would not be a victim of bad traditional beliefs that the musician said degraded women. While some girls did not buy into the idea, Chebet had resolved to concentrate on education.

She did not share this with her mother but wished she could one day share it with the world and take a stand. Could she avoid it now? A pat on her back startled her.

"Hello Cheb. What are you doing here?" she looked at the woman and was at first lost for words. It was Mrs Patricia, a distant relative. Her feet were white with dust and her hands had become rough for working in the quarry.

She was one of the many women who came to work at the quarry. They crushed huge stones into coarse ones and they were paid according to the number of buckets they filled. Chebet knew how this was done and she had come to do the work. It was the only chance she had of making money.

"I have come to look for work," Chebet answered wryly. She then looked away.

Mrs Patricia paused, adjusting the child strapped to her back using a torn, old leso.

"You should have waited Cheb. We just buried your mother yesterday."

Chebet remained quiet.

"You should continue with your studies. This is not the best work."

Chebet gazed at the sky.

"No one will take care of my brothers if I go to school," she answered.

"What about your uncle? He can manage…"

"He can't," she hunched her shoulders. "He cannot manage."

Chebet struggled with tears that threatened to burst into a stream.

Mrs Patricia adjusted the baby on her back again.

Chebet clasped her forehead. She then noticed Mr Chumo, the owner of the quarry, walking towards them. She knew very little about him.

"Young girl, are you looking for work?" he asked while approaching them.

He teased Mrs Patricia's baby. Chebet nodded in silence.

"Are you a pupil?" he asked with concern.

"She is a pupil," Mrs. Patricia cut in, "But for now, you will have to give her a casual job. She is in dire need of a job."

"But she looks very young. I don't think she will have the energy to crush the stones. You do not look strong enough, girl."

"I will. I swear I will do that, sir," Chebet answered.

Mr Chumo looked at her with pity.

"I really need the job."

"It's okay. You will work with Joel's mum. Do you have a hammer, a chisel and a mattock?"

"Yes, but I did not come with them. Can I bring them tomorrow?"

She knew that she could use her father's tools, which lay unused back in the house.

"I will lend you the mattock, for today only. Do you know how much we pay?"

"No," Chebet answered innocently.

"It's ten shillings for every twenty-kilogramme bucket that you fill. Remember not all stones are useful. You will be shown the stones that we use."

"Yes," she responded. "Thank you so much."

"I'm glad you have given this little girl a job."

"Who's the father?" he asked conspiratorially.

"This is Rotich's daughter."

"Rotich? Are you talking of the Rotich who used to work here?"

"Yes, that Rotich. His wife was buried yesterday."

"Yes, I know," Chumo responded.

He looked at her with even more pity. He extended his hand to Chebet while shaking his head in disbelief.

"Are you the first born?"

Chebet nodded.

"Please work with Patricia. She will guide you. If you are like your father, then you will work very hard. He was a very hardworking man," he said.

He asked her to follow Mrs Patricia to a big ditch, where people were working. The walls looked like they could collapse any time. In case the walls collapsed, the people working inside would be buried alive. It happened once when her father was working at the quarry. Fortunately, her father was absent because he was sick. He would have died just like his four friends who were buried alive. After the incident, work at the quarry continued.

A number of women and children were working side by side with more than ten men. Mrs Patricia showed her some of the stones she had gathered so that she could work on them.

"He is bringing you the mattock," Mrs Patricia commented.

Chebet stood there, watching what the other people were doing. She had never done it before, but she vowed to do it. Among the people working, none seemed interested in her. They were just busy.

She noticed two children who had quit school at Class Four and Five recently. They were now experts and they broke the stones without much struggle. There was also a young girl, probably her age, standing next to a boy Chebet thought must be the brother. They put their stones together. At a far corner was another girl of her age, but who Chebet knew was now married to an older man. The girl's belly seemed to have grown bigger and she lazily broke the stones with a hammer. One of her breasts was exposed but she did not seem to mind. She gave Chebet a glance and went on with her work.

"Work with your mother there," Chumo directed her as he gave her the mattock. It was so heavy it almost fell to her feet when she took it into her hands.

"You can work on the stones I have gathered. However, put the stones you have broken down here," she pointed at an empty space.

She observed how Mrs Patricia was doing it. She lifted the heavy mattock and dropped it on the big stone. The stone remained intact; it did not crack a bit.

Chapter Seven

Dennis, Julius and Chebet sat around a big fire feeding it more firewood while hoping that more fire would cook the maize faster as they were all hungry. Despite being allowed in class, the two young boys had spent the day without any food. It was quite late in the night and they had been at the fire for close to two and a half hours waiting for the maize to cook. Chebet had bought half a kilogramme of dry maize with all the money she had made at the quarry. Though it was difficult, she made seventy shillings. She was happy that she got some money but she was exhausted. She was not sure she would have the energy to work the following day. Every part of her body was aching while her hands were full of painful blisters. Her back throbbed with pain as did her hands which could not lift anything heavy. She had also injured her left hand and kept on ignoring the piercing pain. It was a painful and tough start. She sympathised with her father who knew no other place of work but the quarry. He occasionally complained of backache. Chebet did not understand then, but she now knew why. Her father did a most tiring job hence the sicknesses that he was accustomed to. He used to sigh and gasp in pain and tiredness at night. He, however, never stopped working for them, ensuring that they got the basic needs. It was now Chebet's turn.

"Chebet, you are dozing off," Julius laughed.

Chebet opened her eyes. She pushed the firewood deeper into the fire. She did not respond to her brother. She was worn out.

"When people came here, some gave money. Did they give it to you Cheb?" Julius asked.

"I did not see ..." Chebet answered ignorantly, opening the lid that covered the boiling food.

"There was a book where people wrote their names."

"Who took the book?" she asked.

"Uncle Norbert," Julius responded.

Did he also take the money for the party that had been planned to take place after my supposed circumcision? she thought and twisted her mouth in disgust.

"Will you fight if people come to beat us sister?" a worried Dennis asked. He glanced at the darkness that surrounded them. "We do not have anyone else and you told us to leave our uncle's home."

Chebet looked intently at him. She, too, worried that they were the only ones in the compound. No one volunteered to stay with them, apart from her uncle whom she was convinced had ulterior motives. No one offered to take them in. Chebet did not mind this and, though she was usually afraid of darkness, she now had some energy and she thought little of the neighbours eight hundred metres away.

"We shall go back to our uncle's home," Chebet said unconvincingly.

"But you said we shall never go there again Cheb," Dennis commented immediately. "Why did you tell us to leave in the morning?"

"Uncle wants me to get married."

"Shall we go with you if you get married? We cannot stay alone Cheb," Dennis said.

"Why do girls get married early, yet boys are not allowed?" he wondered.

"I will not leave you. We shall stay here on our own. I will work and you will continue with school…" though Chebet pretended to ignore her brother's question, it ate away at her very core.

"Why would girls be married at 12 years, but not boys?" she wondered too.

"But you said we shall go to his home, then…" Julius moaned.

"I said we will stay here on our own. I will continue to work in the quarry and buy food for ourselves. You shall continue with school," she paused, "One day, I will open my quarry and employ people. I will then buy goats and cows to replace the ones we lost to famine."

"Cheb, will you go to school yourself?" Julius asked with concern.

"Yes," she blew her nose, "But it depends. I may never go to school if…" she stopped when tears started falling from her eyes.

"Are you crying, sister?" Dennis asked while sucking on his thumb. "Even Julius is crying."

"I will never go to school. The person who used to take care of us died. Mother then followed. I will work for you but I'm worried that I will die like mother," she sobbed loudly.

She staggered as she rose from the floor and searched for dry leaves with which to remove the cooking pot from the fire.

"God! Why these? Please don't take anyone else," she muttered.

She limped after a couple of minutes and started searching for dry leaves with which to remove the cooking pot from the fire. Dennis followed her, his thumb still in his mouth.

"I'm hungry, Chebet. I want to eat…"

"Didn't you eat at school, Dennis?" Chebet asked as she continued searching for dry leaves, tears drying on her cheeks.

"No, we were late. We were told that we were not included in the list of pupils present."

"So you have not eaten?" she asked with concern, bending down to pick some leaves.

"No. Did you eat at the quarry?" Dennis asked.

"No, I did not have any money to buy food."

She then matched back and took the cooking pot off the fire. She almost dropped it when she heard some noise from the far end of the compound. Dennis grabbed her dress, while Julius stood and watched curiously.

"Someone is standing there," Julius pointed at a part of the dark compound. Chebet looked and an intense fear overwhelmed her. Who would protect them against bad and evil people? She gazed without blinking. Her stomach started to rumble while her knees weakened. Dennis started to cry. Julius covered his mouth, muffling his crying. They waited silently.

"Who are you?" Chebet asked shaking. There was some silence. Her heart thumped heavily.

"Who are you?" she asked again.

They started to retreat back into the house.

"Oh God, please protect us," she prayed silently.

"Do not be worried, my children. It's your uncle."

"What do you want, Uncle?" Chebet asked angrily.

"I'm taking you home. You cannot stay alone like this," he said while approaching them.

"I'm taking the three of you."

"You will take Dennis and Julius. I will not go, Uncle, please…"

"You are all coming with me. Don't be stubborn, Chebet."

She noticed that her uncle was not alone. He had company.

"It's risky to stay here alone," the other person commented. Chebet recognised the voice immediately. It was the old man she was to marry.

"Do they want to marry me off immediately? No way," she vowed to herself.

"Please leave!"

"Chebet, do not act like a mother here, okay? Grab her …" her uncle instructed his friend. Chebet screamed, warning him not to approach her.

"Leave her alone!" Julius held the man by his feet and bit him. Uncle Norbert pushed Julius away, making him fall on the ground like a sack of maize. Chebet wished she could do something to protect her siblings.

Uncle Norbert's friend grabbed her, hurting the already injured hand.

"Leave me alone!" he shouted

"Do not release her, Nicholas," her uncle shouted.

"Are you doing this because our parents are dead?" Chebet protested. She tumbled as she was shoved forward. "You took all the money that was given during the burial preparations. You are a thief…You are…"

Uncle Norbert slapped Chebet so hard that she lost sight of everything for a few seconds. She then gaped at him, her heart boiling with rage.

"I do not entertain nonsense," he roared.

"You will regret doing this, Uncle." Chebet swore silently.

Chapter Eight

Chebet gently pushed away the torn bedsheet that covered the three of them. She stared at her brothers who slept on, unperturbed beside her. Dennis, thumb in mouth, was sprawled on the rickety wooden bed, sound asleep. Julius slept on his side. He moved when Chebet rose from the bed. She stopped. On the other side, her cousin was equally sound asleep. He licked his lips before smiling broadly; the smile visible despite the faint light of dawn. He must have been dreaming because the smile was followed by mumbling. His brown, stained bedsheet was spread out on the ground leaving his dusty feet uncovered. The feet were very dusty, probably carrying all the dust he had gathered while out with their livestock the previous day.

Chebet tiptoed to what was the sitting room. Not a sound was heard when she entered the sitting room since only a leso separated the two rooms. It would have been a totally different case with a squeaky door. She surveyed the room, trying to pick out anything useful. She was not sure what she wanted, but studied the whole room, cautious not to wake her uncle and aunt who slept in the adjacent room. She moved towards an old kitchen cabinet that stood at the corner of the house. She opened the drawers and almost screamed when a rat jumped out of the drawer. She hopped back. Her heart beat faster.

She bit her right-hand pointing finger as if remembering something, before tiptoeing back to the bedroom. She pulled her dress from the hanging line and walked back to the sitting room. It was then that she saw her aunt's handbag.

"Do I take this? Do I leave it?" she thought as she looked at the handbag.

She moved towards it but stopped abruptly when she heard her uncle's voice from the bedroom. He was mumbling something. She thought she heard soft sobbing. Her aunt was sobbing.

"Could they have heard me move?" she wondered.

She hastily took the handbag and quietly opened the main door. She walked out of the house.

It was quiet outside. Cattle lay on the ground chewing their curd a few metres from the house. Her uncle, unlike many in Marigat, still had some livestock.

Chebet broke into a run, away from the house.

"Where am I going?" she asked as doubt threatened to slow her down.

She got to the main rough road, but continued running, the handbag and the dress still in her hands.

She recalled the heated conversation with her uncle the previous night.

"Tomorrow, Nicholas will take you away. He will marry you at a later date. In the meantime, he will take care of you and your brothers. I do not want to hear any nonsense from you. He will have the permission to discipline you accordingly," she winced as she recalled her uncle's words. "If you act childish, he will beat you up."

"Uncle, I'm still young," she pleaded but to no avail.

"Chebet, you will have to learn to respect culture. Through culture, you show respect for the community and your family too. Your mother respected this. Remember: Nicholas will take care of you. But first, you must be circumcised. Your aunt will escort you to the rite tomorrow morning. Several girls and women will accompany you. From there, you will learn how to talk like an adult. People will come in the morning to prepare for the feast that will take place in this homestead. We have put everything in place. I do not expect and will not entertain any letdown. The feast will be held in the evening. I want discipline. Chelimo failed to instill this discipline in you. I will," her uncle retorted.

"I will never get circumcised. Never," she shot back.

"You are going to be circumcised and I will see to it that you are circumcised. It's not what you say but what the community dictates."

"But the community is wrong… What the community dictates is not necessarily true or correct. I will not get circumcised. I will not get married," she had vowed in front of her aunt before matching off to the bedroom. No one followed her but she was sure she saw a hint of approval in her aunt's face. She did not know what her uncle and aunt resolved but she was sure her uncle would forcefully implement his plan. She could not wait for that to happen.

She spent the whole night wondering what to do and where to run. She had initially thought of reporting the matter to the chief but changed her mind because the chief supported the community practices. He participated in celebrations involving circumcision of girls. He did not even oppose the marriages of young girls. She could not, therefore, run to the chief for help.

She stopped on the way and opened the handbag to put in the dress. She noticed a handkerchief that was tied into a knot. She removed the handkerchief and untied the knot. There was money in the knot.

"It is wrong to run away with someone's money. I need to return it," she thought.

She counted the money; it came to nine hundred shillings. She squeezed the notes into her palm, wondering what to do with the money.

"No, I will use this money and one day I will return it," she concluded.

She folded the notes into a nice bundle and put them in the pocket of her dress only to realise that her pocket was torn. She put the money back in the handbag but looked further to see what else was inside. She noticed her aunt's identification card in one of the inner pockets. She could not run away with the identification card.

The roar of a motorcycle engine startled her. She wanted to hide but it was too late. She had been so engrossed in her thoughts that she didn't hear it from a distance. She stood there startled, trembling with fear; either her muscles had stopped aching or she was too busy to think of the ache.

"What if the rider stops and rapes me?" she thought with a shudder.

It was not yet day and the road seemed clear of people. There was a thicket on either side of the road. The dying engine of the motorcycle sent a cold chill down her spine. The rider stopped next to her.

"Are you going to Marigat town?" he asked. She shook her head.

"Okay," he answered but before he set off, Chebet changed her mind and called out.

"Wait! How much?"

"Fifty only."

Chebet sat on the motorcycle awkwardly and injured her hand.

"Where are you going this early?" the rider asked over the roar of the engine. He was not wearing a helmet.

Chebet did not know what to say.

"Nairobi?" he persisted.

"Yes," she responded.

A silence descended between them. Chebet's mind wandered from one thought to another. The man concentrated on his riding on the rough road.

It took over forty minutes to get to Marigat town. The last time she was in the town was a year before. She had come with her mother to sell ten of their cows.

She took out a fifty-shilling note and paid him.

"Do you ply that route?" Chebet asked before the man left.

"Yes, I do. Why?"

"Can I ask for a favour?"

"Sure, you can."

"Would you mind to drop this ID to any home near the place you picked me? It is my aunt's but I took it by mistake."

He took the ID and studied it.

"Why not take it back by yourself?"

"I'm travelling and won't be back soon…"

"Okay," he finally responded to Chebet's great relief.

She remained rooted to the spot wondering where to go. She had never gone beyond Marigat town. She remembered her brothers and guessed that they had woken up. She had not told them about her plan to run away. Sorrow gripped her. She fought back tears. She had cried enough the previous night.

"What will happen to my brothers? Will we ever meet again?

Who will take care of them? Why not just get married and live with them?" she thought with discomfort.

She wiped the thin mucous streaming from her nostrils with the back of her hand. Just then she felt some liquid trickle down her thighs. Had she urinated on herself in the excitement to get away?

She put her hand inside the torn pocket of the dress. She touched a sticky liquid and was extremely shocked at what she saw. It was blood.

"What just happened?" she asked aloud.

She did not feel any pain but something had seriously hurt her. She started trembling with fear and worry.

She checked again and confirmed that it was blood.

"Did anyone do something bad to me? Did the motorcycle hurt me?" she thought, putting her legs together in a bid to stem the flow of blood.

"Aren't girls supposed to ride on a motorcycle?

Just then the blaring of a matatu horn brought her back from her thoughts. She hastily stepped back, almost dropping the handbag.

"Nairobi! Nairobi!" the conductor shouted. "Four hundred shillings only."

The matatu left her even more confused. The driver stopped the vehicle and the conductor alighted.

She started walking towards it.

"Where are you heading to?" she asked the conductor.

"I said Nairobi," he responded. "Are you going to Nairobi?"

Chebet nodded unsurely and immediately boarded the matatu. She sat at the back, close to the window.

Chapter Nine

Excitement, fear, anxiety and sorrow left Chebet confused, even as she stared with curiosity at the beautiful land, houses and people she was seeing along the tarmacked roads. She was sad that she left her brothers without anyone to take care of them. However, she did not know her destination and was not sure of where she was going. She had taken a major risk.

A signpost indicated that Nairobi was fifteen kilometres away, something that made her realise her blunder. She was getting to the city, but did not know where she was going. It was around 2 PM. It would be night in a few hours. She hated to think it would soon be dark. Thinking of this made her forget the wet stream of blood she had stemmed by stuffing her aunt's handkerchief between her thighs. The handkerchief now absorbed the blood, sparing her dress further stains. She felt this was a better though uncomfortable option.

Different thoughts assailed her. She had heard of some aunts who lived in Nairobi but she did not know where. Worse, those relatives hardly came home; they would not recognise her if they saw her.

She held the bag firmly on her lap and wiped away tears from her eyes. She covered her face so that the young man sitting next to her would not notice.

"Can I go back?" Chebet wondered.

Her heart beat faster as if to pave the way for the explosion of her head. Reality was dawning on her that she would be in Nairobi soon.

"Welcome to Nairobi. Do not litter the city," read a signpost that stood next to another that indicated that Nairobi City was ten kilometres away.

She leaned forward on the seat and gave in to the grief that overwhelmed her. She quietly wiped her tears with the back of her hand. The young man sitting next to her seemed to have realised that she was crying but he ignored her. He alighted a short while later.

"I wish I had got married," she regretted. "I would be comfortable at home. I wouldn't worry over a city that I know nothing about. I will go back immediately," she resolved.

Several passengers then alighted at a place she thought was not a bus stop. The matatu stopped on a wide road, which she assumed was Moi Avenue, due to the writing on a metallic post at the junction. Everything was new to her and for the hundredth time, she regretted coming to the city that she only knew by name. She kept on waiting to see if she would get to a field where the buses and matatus parked and waited for passengers.

Contrary to her expectations, people alighted and boarded vehicles at any place, leaving her wondering as to whether there was anything like a bus stop in the city. She noticed a group of people on the road shouting. She did not understand why until she realised they were hawkers selling different wares. The people then ran off carrying their commodities. The boxes they had placed their items on disappeared too. Shortly after, a group of uniformed cops emerged, pursuing the hawkers.

"Was the city this confused and disorderly with so many people walking on the streets? Is it always this busy?" she wondered.

A long queue of vehicles had formed and Chebet realised that the other passengers were alighting. She adjusted the handkerchief she had put between her thighs then alighted. She was perplexed and did not know which direction to take. People walked hastily in all directions. There were other daring persons that walked between the vehicles on the road.

She walked carefully towards the verandah, struggling to get away from the busy people. A woman held her handbag firmly and walked away while looking at Chebet with suspicion. Others followed suit, leaving Chebet wondering what was wrong with her. She moved towards a tall building with walls mounted with mirrors and looked at her image. She was the odd one out with a patched dress. She was barefoot while everyone else was wearing shoes. Her feet were rough with cracked heels. She was embarrassed and wished the ground could open and swallow her up. A guard moved closer and indicated to her to leave the verandah. When she hesitated, the mean-faced guard held a club in his hand menacingly. She walked off and stopped a few strides away from the building.

A couple of people looked at her incredulously and avoided her.

"Do these people think I will steal from them? Is it because I am smelling of sweat or do they take me to be a street girl?" she thought with sadness.

She hated the moment she boarded the vehicle to come to a city she had never visited.

"Why are the city people this inhuman?" she wondered.

She tried to stop a plump elderly woman for help. The woman strode away hastily. Chebet started to weep, loneliness and desperation engulfing her. What did people think of her?

She walked on the pavement with no destination in mind. She thought of her father.

"When you study and pass your exams very well, you will go to work in Nairobi city. You will then be visiting me all the way from Nairobi. The city is very nice. It makes everyone beautiful," her father had said.

"You were wrong, Dad," she muttered. "The city is an inhuman place. A place where people do not care about others; they only mind what they have."

She reached a place where she had to cross the road. Vehicles were driving by fast. She noticed the traffic lights that she learnt about when she was in Class Five. Their teacher had told them that when traffic light is red, vehicles should stop for pedestrians to cross. This was not happening.

"The teacher may have been wrong," she thought.

She stood there for almost twenty minutes, waiting for the vehicles to stop. Other people came and crossed, leaving her behind. It called for a big resolve to cross the road. Her heart thumped heavily as she crossed the road even though she was at the middle of a group of people. She heard some of the elderly women in the group talk about a class they had. She was interested in their conversation and walked behind them unnoticed.

"Did grown-ups in the city go to school?" she asked. "So I will actually go to school in the future," she thought happily.

She followed them all the way to a gate marked "University of Nairobi." She was excited to see the university, which she had only read of in books. She wished she had the opportunity to reach that level of education. It was unfortunate she was now a Class-Six dropout. She doubted whether her brothers would even get to Class Six. Misery had visited them and their chances of going on with their schooling were slim.

She walked past the university for another twenty minutes not knowing where she was headed. As she walked, she kept on confirming that the handkerchief was fine and tight between her legs, even though it was more drenched and difficult to ignore.

She noticed a restaurant across the road. She crossed over and went straight in. She sat down but rose later when she realised no one was coming to attend to her. There was a queue to the cashier. It was then that she saw the "self-service" notice. Those on the queue paid and were served with food. Her surprise was that everyone was eating french fries or chips; a few people took the fries with fried chicken.

"They do not sell ugali? I want ugali," she muttered.

She rose and joined the queue. Chebet noticed that no one came close to her; if anything, most of the people looked at her suspiciously. She did not care.

"I want food," she told the cashier, a young man with a smooth face and big, round eyes.

"Which food? Faster, I have other customers behind you."

She looked at him and was tempted to ask: "Am I not a customer?"

"Ugali."

"I have no time to waste. What do you want, madam?" he asked the next customer, ignoring her.

"Give me those... " Chebet pointed at the fries. The cashier looked at her with cold eyes.

She moved after getting the change and was served with fries wrapped in a polythene paper. She expected to be served on a plate but realised that everyone in the restaurant was eating their food from polythene papers.

She dug into the chips greedily, never mind that they were without salt. She did not know that there was salt, tomato sauce and pepper at the tables that she should have put in her polythene paper of French fries.

After her meal, she asked for water but was told she had to pay for it. All the bottled water sitting invitingly on the shelves behind the cashier was for sale.

"Is water a rare commodity in this big city, too?" she wondered.

She bought a bottle of water and took time to read the writings on the bottle.

She walked out later and crossed the road. She walked until she reached a garden, where people lay on grass. A billboard identified the garden as Uhuru Park. She walked into the park and fearfully sat under a tree. She was surprised by the sight of the numerous tall buildings to the south of the park.

The sun was not far from setting. She recalled her brothers back at home and thought over the uncertainty of both her life and theirs. She thought of the distance that separated them and wondered what could be happening to them. Memories of her mother came alive and she started to feel hatred well up inside her.

Why did you propose things without telling me, Mother? Why did you tell Uncle to marry me off? Why, Mother, when you knew that I wanted to study? Now my life is ruined and you are not there for us, Mother, why? she thought as tears flowed freely on her cheeks.

"Mother, I will take care of my brothers but I swear I will not get married at my age. No, I will not," she vowed silently.

She felt so tired. The hope she had was now gone; she did not know where life was headed. The future was as bleak as the approaching night was dark. She did not want to think that poverty would forever accompany her. Night would soon fall but she did not know what she was going to do or where she was going to sleep. She was miles away from her orphaned home; far away from the place where she knew people and where, though poor, she had a place to spend the night. She could not talk to her brothers and encourage them. She had deserted them and had gone against the counsel of her mother. What would happen to them?

She looked up in the sky and wondered if there was a god for children and the suffering.

She lay on the grass and closed her eyes. She ignored some street children who sat some distance from where she was. She thought of a lot of things for a few minutes before she fell into a deep sleep and forgot about everything.

Chapter Ten

Thousands of spectators stood cheering the competitors. Some participants wore shorts and sleeveless T-shirts while the others were in ordinary clothes. There were more than fifty athletes and they all seemed convinced that they would win the 10,000 metres race. The venue of the event had a difficult name, which Chebet could not recall.

She stood still behind everyone else. She was the youngest among the participants and felt like withdrawing from the race. However, people from her division cheered her up and encouraged her to participate. A woman who appeared familiar and wore a white dress, gave her a thumbs-up sign. She did not take her eyes off her. Her gaze was very sharp. She felt it penetrate deep into her spine. Next to the woman were some famous people she had met. They, too, flashed her a victory sign.

The whistle was blown and the race started. She stumbled and fell on the ground, injuring her arm. She felt a sharp pain. She held her arm in pain and felt like crying. She had also injured her thigh resulting in a small but painless cut that started to bleed right away. She stared at the blood in shock. She wiped it gently with the other arm.

"Milcah! Milcah! Milcah!" the spectators shouted in unison, clapping their hands rhythmically.

She stole a glance at the excited crowd. She then looked at the participants who were now at the first bend of the track.

"Milcah! Milcah! Milcah!"

She rose from the ground and felt the heavy blouse she was wearing slide off. It felt like someone was removing it from her body. She did not resist. She was left with a camisole.

"Marigat Express! Marigat Express!" the crowd changed the words in their cheer in reference to her home.

The woman dressed in white robes cheered with so much enthusiasm. She felt energy flow into her muscles. It was not the first time she had participated in athletics, more specifically in the long races.

She started to run and picked up speed as she moved on. She caught up with some people after the first lap. Everyone was cheering her up and the attention of the crowd was on her as she overtook the athletes one after the other. She was exhilarated and did not fail to look at the familiar woman in robes. Her breathing was even but her heart beat faster.

On the fifth lap, she was in the lead and no one could keep up with her pace.

"Marigat Express! Marigat Express!" they continued shouting.

She smiled broadly as she led in the last lap, the nearest person coming in more than eighty metres behind. Everybody was clapping to her every step. She was too excited to notice her brothers cheering her up.

"For your brothers," she muttered as she approached the finish line. "I'm doing this for you."

When she hit the finish line, the stadium burst into applause. Her brothers came to hug her.

"You are the best gift to our family and to the whole of Kenya, Sister."

She smiled.

She then noticed her mother approach with her usual smile.

"I knew you would make it girl… Take care of your brothers with the money you will get from the award."

"Mother! Mother!" she started running towards her, forgetting her exhaustion.

Her mother stopped.

"You won the race!"

"Mother! Mother!" she continued shouting, tears cascading down her cheeks. She started running to her, ignoring the officials who wanted to present her with the award for winning the race. Her mother started to run away instead.

"Mother!" she called as she followed her. She ran out of the field, running as if she were flying. When they reached the road outside the stadium, her mother stood in the middle.

"Take care of your brothers, girl."

"No, mother!" she shouted, noticing a lorry approach at high speed. The lorry hit her, throwing her into the air. Chebet was so terrified she could not move. Her hand twitched with pain. Her thighs were soaked in the blood from the cut she sustained in the race. She opened her mouth but no words came out.

"Mother!" she screamed.

Chapter Eleven

Chebet opened her eyes in utter shock. Her left hand throbbed with pain while her thighs were wet. She studied the surroundings and realised she was alone. Night had already fallen but powerful lights on tall posts lit up the whole ground. She rose from the ground, scared and unsure of her location.

"What happened to me?" she asked but soon recalled how she came to the strange place and how she had fallen asleep.

"Ooh! My God!" she mumbled.

She had come with a handbag but it was nowhere to be seen.

"Where is my handbag?

She recalled the stories she had heard about the numerous thieves in Nairobi; that people could steal your socks off your feet and leave your shoes intact.

"No!" she muttered, not believing that her bag could have been stolen.

"Mother… My bag!" she started to weep, clasping her hands behind her head.

"Mother… My bag…"

She started to walk down the park slowly but with despair. This was the end of the world. She regretted a million times why she had come to Nairobi.

"Why is life this unfair? Why all these? Why?" she asked.

She came across a storeyed block and stopped. There were beautiful carvings on a pentagon structure. The powerful lights on one of the tall metallic posts just next to the structure lit up the cemented ground. She could not tell the time. She did not have a watch. She did not have anything. What pained her most was the money that was stolen with the handbag. She could not go back home as there was no fare. She was at point zero.

"The darkest hour is just before dawn," she recalled the words of the celebrated woman from Marigat.

"My parents rejected me and threw me out of the house. I became a streetgirl. However, I never lost focus. Even when I became a housegirl, I did not give up. My determination to improve my life stayed."

She sat on the block, tears streaming down her face.

"It doesn't matter where you come from. Success depends on the determination of a person. From you, I see a great future for the people of Marigat."

She stared at the blurry sky and memories wrestled in her mind. She recalled the chat with the celebrated woman from Marigat. Chebet had been informed by her teachers that she had emerged in position one in the whole of Baringo District.

"When you recited the poem for us, I couldn't stop saying that you have a bright future. Do not let anyone take that potential away," the woman had said.

She gasped with sorrow. Her future was being taken away now and she wondered if she would ever make it. As her classmates said she could not continue with her education, even though she was the brightest pupil in Class Six.

She sobbed uncontrollably. When she stopped, she put her hand in her pocket for the unending and perplexing wetness. She removed the handkerchief and was agitated by what she saw under the bright light. The handkerchief was full of blood.

"What is happening to me?" she wondered aloud.

She did not take witchcraft seriously but this unexplained bleeding had her worried.

"Whom can I tell about these occurrences?"

She held the handkerchief with her right hand, ignoring the blood that soaked it. It slowly dripped to the floor. She noticed a large pool of water a few metres from where she sat. Boats were parked beside the pool. Numerous people passed by the pool but no one seemed to guard it.

"Is this a dam in the city?" she thought aloud.

She moved towards it, not minding blood on her thighs. When she reached the pool she studied it for a few minutes before immersing the handkerchief in it. A deep, menacing voice boomed from a corner.

"Get out of there!"

She stood up and looked at the direction of the voice.

"Get out of there!" The owner of the voice, a man in a blue uniform, shouted at her.

The man threw a stone at her. The stone missed her and fell in the pool, splashing her with water. She ran off.

She reached a structure, which had a statue with a water fountain. She stood and, pretending to put her hand in the pocket, inserted the wet handkerchief between her thighs. As she was doing it a shabby teenager approached her. He held a bottle, stuck to his nose.

"Welcooome si-s-ter," he slurred.

Chebet stared at him, wondering what he had drunk; must be one of the street children, high on glue.

The boy moved closer to her.

"You are big like me," the boy said and stretched an arm to touch her breasts, something that irked Chebet to no end. She slapped him in the face. The boy only laughed awkwardly and, undeterred, stretched his hand towards her breasts.

"Silly!" Chebet shouted as she started running away from the boy. He laughed out loud.

Chebet ran up a sloppy ground. Her legs were aching by the time she got to the top. She stopped to catch her breath. She faced the direction she had come from and stared blankly at the well-lit city buildings.

"Mother, she is a street girl. I have seen her running. She is looking at your handbag," a girl warned a woman she was with.

"I'm not a thief and I'm not a street child," she shouted back furiously.

The mother and child took to their heels, leaving Chebet even more annoyed. She walked away to a different place in the park. Memories of her brothers came alive and a thin flow of mucous ran down her nostrils. She fought back tears of anguish.

"Why all these? My father died; then my mother. Now I have left school because no one seems to care for us. I have no one to run to. I have no money. Where will I go now? Where is God in all these? God hates my family because we do not go to church. Why doesn't He help us if He loves us? What will I do now? God, what will happen to my life?" she muttered.

She felt weak and dizzy. Her vision was becoming blurred.

"What is happening to me?"

She tried to support herself by leaning on a tree but her shaking legs gave way and she slid to the ground, losing consciousness. Her body started to jerk involuntarily.

Everything became dark.

Chapter Twelve

Grace listened carefully. She heard someone's footsteps accompanied by soft sobs which she believed came from either Dennis or Julius. The two had been weeping all day asking for their sister as if Grace and her husband knew her whereabouts. It had been a long day. They had looked everywhere for the girl. It took them almost ten hours to conclude that she had probably travelled to Nairobi. Grace was very disturbed. Did she know anyone in the city? What would become of her?

She moved from the bed and trod lightly towards the sitting room. She was worried and feared Dennis and Julius would run away too. The most probable person who could disappear was Dennis whom she viewed as very bright, just like her sister. She would not want to be blamed for worsening the lives of the desperate children. She had tried to stop her husband from forcefully marrying off Chebet but to no avail.

She knew the pains of early marriages for she was a victim - she was married at only thirteen years and gave birth a year later. The baby died after a few months. She had always regretted that and wished she could turn back her life and say no to that.

Her life in marriage was characterised by so much suffering that she had lost interest in it. She now lived by the day with no excitement about the next day.

Her reproductive system was affected terribly. The doctor carried out tubal ligation some years later; she could not conceive any more. Her uterus and urinary bladder became worse when she gave birth to her only son. She could not control her bladder and easily passed urine on herself, something that kept her away from other women. When this happened, her husband ran to his other wives. The doctor said that she was suffering from urinary incontinence, something that was brought about by her early pregnancy. It was argued that the increased weight on a uterus that was not yet formed properly and the stress of her reproductive organs during delivery weakened the muscles required for bladder control.

This happened when she gave birth to the first child. The baby died later because of the stress it faced at delivery. She was lucky to have survived. Later, she had numerous miscarriages, until she gave birth to her one and only son.

When the incontinence started, the doctor prescribed tubal ligation, something her husband was not happy about. He still talked of it, especially when he got angry or drunk. Grace lived with this guilt and shame. She feared interacting with other people because of the incontinence. She was thus elated when Chebet resisted to be married at an early age; she had silently wished that Chebet could reject the offer. She could not talk openly about this because she feared her authoritarian husband. She was happy that

Chebet had disappeared; that is why she did not feel so terrible that in the bag that Chebet had taken was her money. Her only worry: Where was she? Who would take care of her?

She opened the door and saw Dennis in the darkness. He stood at the door sobbing softly.

"Dennis," she called while moving towards him. She held his shoulders tenderly. "Chebet will come back, I know where she went. She will come back," she whispered.

"I want to stay with her… I wanted to go with her…" Dennis commented while weeping.

"It's okay," she patted his back lovingly, not seeing his sorrowful face in the dark. "Chebet will come back for you."

"Where did she go?"

She paused confusedly.

"Chebet went to look for work so that she may take care of you."

"What's happening there?" her husband asked in a sleepy voice.

They both kept quiet.

"I am asking. What's happening there? Can you go to sleep?"

No one responded.

"Did Uncle chase Chebet away?" Dennis asked.

"No," she answered with hesitation. "Will you now go to sleep," she pleaded. Dennis hesitated.

"Who will be taking care of us? Shall we go to our home?"

"Why, Dennis?"

"I don't want to stay here. I want to stay at our home," he responded frankly.

"It's okay, Dennis. Please go and sleep, now."

He moved back to their bedroom.

Grace remained standing at the door. She pitied the children and worried about their future. One thing she knew was that they could not afford to stay in her house. Her husband would definitely clash with them because he would not know how to handle them.

She sighed in confusion, shaking her head thoughtfully. If she had the ability she would take care of them. The best she could do was pray for them. She went back to her bedroom befuddled and concerned.

"May God protect these children. May He protect Chebet, wherever she is," she muttered sorrowfully.

She lay on the bed and continued thinking.

"Why does God allow some people to suffer? Why would an innocent child suffer, when he or she has done nothing wrong? Why would God let innocent children become orphaned then leave them to suffer? Was anything good lying ahead in their life?" she thought with agony.

She recalled what someone once told her about pain being a source of wisdom and that it made people more human. The pain and suffering that one undergoes determines how interesting one's life becomes. Maybe the pain and suffering the children were undergoing will one day make them better persons and their story day be told will one.

She closed her eyes and said a prayer for the three orphans.

Chapter Thirteen

The cold and misty wind blowing along the road made her shiver. Her mouth shuddered of its own accord. A severe headache nagged her. She felt tired of wiping off the cold mucous with the back of her hands. She did not want to use the short blanket that a Good Samaritan had given her. The tea she had been given was not good enough to warm her up. She cleared it in a few gulps and prayed silently that the Good Samaritan could extend his generosity and add another cup. She was hungry and thirsty but shy to ask for food from the old man who worked as a guard in the first building facing what she saw was Nairobi University. He was a kind man.

She stared at the numerous stars in the sky that seemed to communicate an end of the world. Her look would have been mistaken for that of someone who had seen something interesting or one reading some inscriptions in the sky. She felt like she was seeing her mother looking at her.

"You told me you left Marigat for Nairobi where you don't know anyone? Strange my daughter," the old man with brown and broken teeth said.

Chebet looked at him.

"Yes. We were left with no one. My uncle wanted me to get married," she paused. The old man put the thermos flask into a black bag. There was some tea remaining and Chebet wished he could give it to her. She fell short of making the request.

"Where will you go when morning comes?" he finally asked, his hands covered by the woollen socks he wore as gloves. His heavy overcoat which must have kept him very warm, made him look plump but his lean face gave him away. He was a thin man.

Chebet looked at him before diverting her attention far away to Koinange Street. The scantily dressed young women who had earlier lined up along the street were slowly disappearing. The girls had shocked her with their manner of dressing. She noticed how they called for the attention of men, especially those who drove by. The girls cat-walked seductively whenever a vehicle appeared. Chebet had seen some of them board the vehicles which were then driven off. The whole episode was scandalous and Chebet felt so ashamed.

"Why do they do that?" she asked herself.

One of the girls had come to the place they were sitting and changed from decent clothes into very scanty ones. She seemed not to mind changing clothes on the streets, specifically in front of a man of her grandfather's age. She joked lightly as she changed into her work clothes, stuffing the decent clothes into a polythene bag.

"You decided to come with your granddaughter. Want to

orient her to this business?" the lady had asked in a hoarse voice. She was naked save for a tiny strip of cloth that passed for her underwear. She was of medium size and her long legs shone with oil. Her breasts were quite big and round.

"Can you orient her?" the man had asked. "You can be her teacher, you know."

"Please don't. It's not the best of work. She cannot cope with the harshness of men."

She had then marched away proudly, a cigarette in her hands. Her back was bare while her breasts threatened to burst out of the little blouse she wore.

The lady had not come back for the clothes she left with the old man. Chebet was shy to ask the old man about the girls. For the few hours she had spent with the old man, she had not asked anything to do with them though curiosity burned up inside her.

"I don't know where I will go," she said once gain looking at the old man. She had trusted him despite his interaction with the prostitute. He had remained with her blue jeans and the long silk top she had been wearing.

"I want to go back," she mumbled.

The old man remained quiet. Chebet hoped he would say something. She gazed at the junction where a vehicle had stopped. The girl was dropped off and she walked towards them, lighting a cigarette as soon as she alighted.

"Good deal for the night," she said drunkenly when she got to the place they were sitting. "Men think they are wise, but we are wiser than them, young girl."

She staggered as she took her trousers from the polythene paper placed next to the old man's stuff. She then took off the extremely short skirt. Chebet looked away in shame when the woman bent down and exposed her back.

"Why lose dignity this much?" Chebet asked silently.

"Are you shy my dear?" the woman patted Chebet.

Chebet did not say anything. She looked at the sky, wondering why some things happen in life.

"I will never become a prostitute," she vowed.

Though there were streetlights all over, Chebet noticed that dawn was approaching and the girls were slowly leaving the streets. Their day was done.

"Tomorrow," she said after dressing decently. "I'm the good girl now; the mother of Marion." With that, she walked away.

"No matter the problems you may face, never ever dream of doing what these girls do," the old man said after the woman had disappeared from view.

"Their actions degrade them so much and they lose their dignity for money. It will feel good to succeed in activities that you can proudly tell people about. If you can tell people about your success story without any guilt or shame, then you have a nice story. But if you succeed through evil schemes, then your story can only be told in shame and guilt. Let your story be a genuine one." He shook his head with sadness. Chebet listened, not knowing how to respond.

"I know you are facing serious problems, particularly after losing your parents at your age. Despite this, do not engage in evil practices thinking it will relieve you of all your pain. It may reduce your financial problems. Unfortunately, it will triple your guilt and shame. It's better to deal with pain than guilt and shame," he looked away. "They smoke, get drunk and take drugs to get through what they are doing. It's very wrong. Live with your dignity, my daughter. It's loose morals that lower someone's dignity not poverty."

Chebet struggled to understand the wisdom of the old man. There was some silence between them for a few minutes.

She recalled how she ended up meeting the old man. She had woken up feeling very weak and realised she was alone in the park. A cold wind had left her shaking. It appeared like it was addressed to her as a visitor. She had walked out of the park on to the verandah; that is where she had met the old man who, unlike other people, listened to her. He had advised her to stay with him until morning. Morning was approaching and she felt confused, not knowing what to do.

"I'm sorry, but…" she paused.

"What?" the old man asked with concern.

"Will you lend me money?"

"What for?"

Chebet went quiet. Her heart was pounding with so much fear that she felt the wetness of the handkerchief between her legs.

"I want to go back to Marigat. I cannot stay here anymore. Life is very difficult here. I have nothing and…" she stopped.

The old man was quiet for a while.

"I don't have any money," he said, breaking her heart. "You see, we spend the night in the cold, but what do we get my daughter? Nothing. I wish I had the money."

She felt like crying. He must have noted how frustrated she became after he told her that he did not have money.

"We can wait for the morning. I may get some money from my boss, okay?"

Chebet nodded with excitement. She wanted to talk, but she did not know what to say. She looked up at the sky and smiled.

About an hour later, a black Mercedes Benz pulled over in front of them. The lights were put off immediately and the driver took sometime before alighting. The old man stood up and walked towards the vehicle. Its door opened and a tall woman alighted, an expensive looking handbag in her hands. The old man saluted her respectfully.

"Who are you and what do you want here?" she asked in a harsh voice. Chebet stood up not knowing what to say or how to respond. She looked at the old man, expecting him to respond on her behalf.

"Who is this?" she asked the old man.

The old man narrated Chebet's story to her. Chebet was happy that she was listening though she noted that the old man was trembling like a reed.

"She needs fare to go back to her home," he concluded.

"How much?" she asked callously.

"I don't know." Chebet responded.

"Aren't these lies little girl? You have fabricated a story so that you can con people money, right?"

"No madam, I cannot do that," she pleaded.

"Don't you wear shoes? Do we still have people who do not wear shoes?"

"You know…"

"Shhhhh, I'm not interested," she cut in rudely.

"I will call you. I'm not sure I want you in my office with those dusty feet and that stinking smell. Don't you bathe?"

"I do."

"And?" she looked at her with very cold eyes. Chebet was worried and she looked at the old man.

"I will call you," the woman told the old man.

She walked leisurely into the corridor.

"I don't think she will give me money. She hates me," Chebet commented desolately, fighting back tears.

"I did not choose to be born in a remote area, to poor parents," she protested silently.

"Why do people hate me and others run away from me? Is it because I am stinking, or is it because I do not have shoes and have an old, patched dress?"

She waited for an answer from the old man.

"That doesn't matter. What matters is how you are going to live your life," he responded.

"You did not respond to my questions. Are you feeling irritated by me?"

The old man shook his head. Chebet looked away. She started to sob quietly.

Chapter Fourteen

Rosemary sat low and comfortable on her leather office seat. She swung her feet proudly, a pen in her mouth. A file lay open on the beautiful, brown mahogany table. There was an expensive notebook at the edge of the table and a pen holder she was given as a gift by a United Arab Emirates company when she visited them last month in Dubai.

She pulled the notebook and jotted something in it. She then flipped another page on the file, studied it and signed. It was a contract that was done by the family lawyer, in reference to a plot of land she had purchased in Lavington Estate. One of many such properties she had bought. Since she resigned from her job as a bank manager three years ago, she had ventured into real estate, rapidly growing an empire. However, she felt there was still much to do and had to keep on getting more. Her husband, an engineer with a Chinese firm, supported this and contributed towards the investments. It had been two months since she had the time to together with her husband to talk. She had also not managed to spare time for her three children. Her friend was telling her that when parents get sucked into the business of being very busy and lack time with their children, then their children lack models to emulate and get confused as far as their sexual and psycho-social development is concerned. In other words, they get confused personalities and identities.

Rosemary was not sure of this, but she seemed to agree after her sister refused to stay with her three children when they visited over the weekend. She said Rosemary's children were ill-mannered and would spoil her children. She described them as very rough, mannerless and with no feelings for others. Though this pained her and made her confront her sister, she now seemed to believe it especially after finding her 12-year son browsing inappropriate internet sites the previous evening. Rather than study for his exams, he was busy with the phone she bought him. She did not know what to do or what to tell him. Rosemary just took away the phone but her son, Jean, was not bothered. Rosemary had concluded that the housegirl had introduced her son to such sites. She chased her away immediately. Rosemary suspected the housegirl because she once found pornographic movies in her bag. When she asked about them, Jean took the housegirl's side and dared Rosemary to chase the housegirl away. Rosemary ignored the issue. She could not ignore it yesterday and did not care where the housegirl would go at that late hour of the night. She threw out all her belongings. The housegirl picked them up as she walked out of the compound, accompanied by the guard.

She perused another page and signed. She leant on the seat and swung her feet some more.

"I will take this girl for a month only. She is very shady but she can be taught a few things. She can assist Roselita for the time being. I will, however, have to employ a learned person to take care of my children, someone who can help them with homework. That girl, filthy as she may be, looks bright," she thought.

Roselita was the woman who came to assist in the compound, particularly in washing clothes. That day, Rosemary had instructed her to come early so that she could prepare her children for school.

"But I cannot stay with her. She cannot sleep in my compound. Roselita will have to go with her to her home. I will make it clear that she shouldn't wash the clothes, or cook food for my children. She can only clean the compound, feed the cows and goats and maybe, wash the utensils. No, she will break the utensils."

A phone call interrupted her thoughts.

"Good morning Rosemary," her friend spoke from the other end of the line, "How is your schedule today? Can we meet at 9 PM?"

"Of course, we can," she replied.

"Let's meet at the place we were last month, on Mombasa Road. There is a deal I want us to discuss."

"Okay, cheers," she said and hung up.

She then summoned the guard to bring Chebet.

Chebet and the old man entered her office, the latter trailing the former. It was a sight she hated but had to put up with, just this once.

"I'm calling my driver to come pick you up. What is your name again?" she asked.

"Chebet."

"You will assist in my house for a month. A month only... I cannot give you money for nothing. You will work for it. After one month, I will pay you and hope to God I never see your sorry self again, okay? Nothing comes for free. Roselita will have to get you somewhere to stay for the month. Not in my house."

"O-k-a-y," she stammered an answer.

"If you go there and steal, I will get you and..."

"I can never steal, Madam," she paused, seeming to conceal something. "I'm not a thief..."

"Everyone says so. My driver will pick you up shortly. Wait at the gate," she waved Chebet and the old man away.

"Make sure to bathe, do you hear? You smell worse than a rotten skunk. Your feet have already soiled my carpet!"

The girl looked at the carpet. Rosemary was irritated by the girl's foul smell. The old man was no better. As soon as they left, she opened the window wider and sprayed all over the office. She then pulled the magazine that she had purchased the previous day. She flipped through the pages to her page of interest.

"Does your mother or father fail to create time for you? Are they so busy that you see them once in a while? Do you do your homework with your househelp because your father and mother are absent? Is the househelp the person you are close to? If your answers are yes, then..."

She closed the magazine and sunk deeper into the posh seat again. She threw the magazine into the dustbin, even without reading the article to the end. She rose from the seat and stretched. She seriously needed to take breakfast.

Chapter Fifteen

Chebet remained quiet in the backseat. She was so nervous that she did not look out of the window and, therefore, missed out on the beautiful sights along the road. She did not move any of her limbs, fearing that a single movement could trigger a wrong reaction. When she boarded the car, she did not know what happened, but the window wound up automatically. Then she heard a click on the doors, something she did not understand. The driver did not seem to like her and tried to interrogate her, seeking to know where they met with Madam Rosemary and why she was going to her home. He speculated that she was from a very poor family and was being assisted. Chebet acted like she did not understand anything. She had an ill feeling towards the driver, after he asked whether Chebet would board the car with her foul smell. Rosemary had hesitated before permitting her to board. He was then instructed to hand her over to Roselita.

She waited anxiously. She looked at her dusty, dirty feet and felt even more embarrassed. She had transferred some of the dirt and dust from her feet to the carpet in the car. She hoped and prayed that her wetness had not seeped into the expensive car seats. She clasped her hands in fear and glanced at the beautiful mansions that had stone perimeter walls. There were green trees on each compound. Guards stood by each gate.

"How many worlds are there?" she thought quietly. "How does it feel to live in these mansions while others live in shanties? Why do we live in these separate worlds? Is this part of Kenya? Why can't these people come and assist people in Marigat?" she bit her lower lip. "If I ever get money, I will assist the poor. I will assist those living in the poor areas of Marigat. Those who know nothing but the cows."

The car stopped at a black metallic gate. Someone peeped through a hole before opening the gate. A lawn of flowers decorated the pathway to the compound with lights that Chebet thought were unimportant lined up along the driveway.

"I cannot enter here," she said as she looked at her feet pitifully.

"I want to alight," she told the driver who was chatting with the guard in vernacular, probably backbiting her. The guard shot her a look of disdain.

"You will wait here at the gate. At least you know that this home will feel like vomiting if it sees you." Chebet remained quiet. She had seen and heard enough. His insults did not move her.

She waited for him to open the door as she did not have an idea of how to open it. She almost fell on the ground as she was alighting. She looked back and thought she saw some wetness on the seat. Her heart beat faster as she walked with her legs together to conceal the wetness. She felt uneasy. She was also very hungry but could not ask anyone for food.

"You will wait here young girl. Someone will come for you," the driver said as he drove into the compound.

"Go back there. Outside the gate," the guard ordered her. Chebet stared at him in disgust.

"I will actually be happy there," she responded rudely. The guard closed the gates as soon as she stepped out.

Chebet studied the area with curiosity and trepidation. She noticed that there were no people walking along the road. People drove large vehicles.

She walked towards the main road. She noticed a piece of cloth lying in the trench but just as she stretched her hand to pick it up, a voice from behind stunned her into inactivity. She looked back and saw an elderly woman in sandals and a wet frock standing at the gate. She must have been washing clothes or utensils. She had a kind face. Finally, a rose among thorns.

"How are you little girl?" she greeted her. Chebet felt like a human being.

"Fine," she responded. The woman moved towards her and shook hands with her. Chebet felt uncomfortable, wishing to move back a few steps just in case this kind woman, too, got repulsed by her foul stench.

"Please God, don't let her despise me too. Please God," she said a silent prayer.

"Please come with me," the woman said while holding Chebet's hands. The guard seemed to obstruct them.

"You can call Jean's mother if you are in doubt," the woman told the guard.

Chebet did not know how to respond. She followed the woman along the beautifully tarmacked pathway. She was feeling uneasy, what with the blood streaming down her thighs. Any moment now, she feared, the blood would pour down her tattered dress onto the pathway.

"Auntie," Chebet stopped her, "I'm not comfortable coming here. I just want …"

"Shhhh, you are with me. You look very hungry. I will fix you a hot meal."

Chebet did not respond to this but smiled inwardly.

Why is this woman so generous? She asked herself.

Chebet was in awe when she saw the posh house. She wondered how many people lived in the building.

She followed the woman and was directed to sit on a wooden chair outside the house next to a pruned hibiscus. The woman entered the house and came out carrying food. Chebet did not wait to be invited.

"Did someone tell you about me?" Chebet asked as she wolfed down the food. She ignored the spoon but the woman who she learnt was Roselita, advised her to use it. She had never used a spoon.

"I was informed briefly about you. Are you bleeding my dear?"

Chebet stopped eating and looked at the woman frightfully. She shook her head dismally.

The woman stared at her pitifully. "What happened?"

"I rode on a motorcycle yesterday then…"

"Did you fall off the motorcycle?"

Chebet shook her head.

"Did anyone hurt you?"

"No, I saw the blood after I got off the motorcycle," she answered, placing the plate of food on the ground. She had stopped eating.

"Please eat. Finish up the food then I prepare a warm bath for you," Roselita commented.

"What happened to you and what did you do, to the extent that Jean's mother said you come here for a month and earn your fare?" she asked curiously.

Chebet stared blankly at the whispering monk tree standing a few metres away. She then shook her head and started weeping. The plate of food dropped from her hands. Neither of them picked it up. She started to narrate her story even as tears continued to bathe her face. It was more like her few days of infamy. Roselita was unable to control herself. She wiped tears off her wrinkled cheeks as she listened.

Chapter Sixteen

Chebet admired Roselita's single room. There were three wooden seats placed next to the wall facing what was the kitchen; just a space set aside for cooking. A big basin had most of Roselita's utensils placed on a small wooden stool. A paraffin stove lay on the floor next to a lamp with a broken glass. A curtain separated what was a sitting room from the bedroom. A small radio lay at the edge of the bed. There were no signs of a child in the house, something that puzzled Chebet but she did not want to ask.

She occupied one of the wooden seats after wearing a dress a size too large but which she did not mind.

"We shall go back to Rosemary's place to finish up the house chores," she directed Chebet who stood up immediately.

She felt a little more comfortable after the shower. Roselita talked to her about the blood and advised her about what to do anytime it occurred. She told her that it would come every month and that she needed to prepare herself for it. Chebet was embarrassed that no one had told her about that and she had been ignorantly thinking that she was hurt.

They left the house with Roselita. Chebet studied the compound, noticing the rows of houses. Behind the houses were toilets and bathrooms. Chebet had spent quite some time in the toilet before she entered the bathroom. She realised she had not passed urine for several hours and the sight of the toilets escalated the urge to urinate – she felt like she would urinate even before she opened the toilet door.

"The majority of residents here work in the estate. They work for the rich people during the day and come back here in the evening. These shanties are basically squatters," Roselita informed Chebet, just before they sat on the motorcycle back to Rosemary's house.

It took less than twenty minutes to reach Rosemary's compound. They entered the compound, not saying anything to the guard. Chebet walked uncomfortably in the sandals that Roselita had given her. For one, she was not used to wearing shoes. Two, the sandals were a size too large. She knew she looked funny in the large free dress and the large sandals; that did not worry her much now that she had someone taking care of her.

"We shall weed the flower gardens," Roselita told Chebet. "Do you know how to weed?" she asked.

"I have never done so. We don't have land to cultivate at our place. We only keep cattle. But I will do it," she responded.

Roselita entered a small house next to the main house.

"Does someone sleep there?" Chebet asked.

"No, it's a store."

Chebet was shocked. She could not believe that such a good house could be used as a store.

Roselita came out with two pangas and showed her how to weed.

"Do you have children, Aunt?" she asked Roselita innocently.

"Yes, four children," she responded while removing mud from her panga.

"But I did not see them. Are they in school?"

"Yes, they are in school, but they stay with their father in Roysambu."

Chebet was confused.

"You do not stay with them?"

"No, I stay on my own and they stay with their father. You see, when you grow up, you will learn so many things. You will learn that money is very good but it can be the worst devil in the world. You will also learn that most people become very proud when they gain wealth. They think that money is the highest and biggest thing and that you have a right to do anything once you have it. You mistakenly think that money can buy happiness, love and peace. It then makes you forget the people who helped you achieve that wealth. You get other people who would want to share in your wealth and hard work. Men get other eyes and think that they have the money to buy young and beautiful girls. Money… Money can be a devil. Someone said that money is the devil's excrement. Unfortunately, it is required in God's land as manure.

It depends on how you view and take it. Faeces or manure... My dear, you have a life to live and you have not yet faced anything. You told me your tale of sorrow. What I will tell you is that life is very unpredictable. It's good to be open to face whatever may happen; irrespective of what happens, life has to go on. Be open for anything. My husband married a very young woman who is now building houses for her family from the money she siphons off my husband." She then bent down and started weeding. Chebet gazed at her, trying to take in all that Roselita had mentioned.

"Do they visit you? The children?" she asked.

She rose again, a hard expression on her face.

"Their father cannot let them see me. But I know it's not him. He would wish to but the young woman cannot let this happen. She uses the children as bait and she is able to have all the trust from my husband. She gives the impression that she loves them very much. But I know it's all pretence," she responded with sadness. "The stepmother is very wise. By the time he realises what is happening, it will be too late."

Chebet remained quiet.

"You did not get another husband?" Chebet asked. Roselita smiled.

"Life is not all about having a man. It's about being happy and being at peace with yourself and your neighbour."

Chebet thought of her parents and wondered.

"How can children abandon their mother who is actually alive and choose to live with a stepmother? Did they do that because their mother was not learned and did not have money? How can that happen?" Chebet wondered.

She continued with her effort to weed. It was too much to understand.

"Be open for anything," Roselita had told her.

They weeded for two hours before they left to prepare tea for Rosemary's children who were about to return from school.

"How does it feel to take care of someone else's children while yours are being taken care of by someone else?"

"It feels bad but life has to go on, my girl."

Chebet followed Roselita into a room whose purpose she did not know. She only guessed it was a kitchen when she noticed utensils on the wooden shelves. She dreaded touching anything and watched as Roselita did the duties.

Roselita prepared tea and put it in very beautiful flasks. She then took it to where she said was the sitting room. Roselita joined her later and sat on a plastic chair, just like the one Chebet was sitting on.

They had become friends and Chebet was at ease talking to her. She realised that Roselita was a good woman and mother. Chebet hated Roselita's children for abandoning her and living with a woman who was not their mother. Roselita said her children termed her shady and did not want to associate themselves with her.

"Someone said that you cannot choose where to be born. You

cannot choose who will be your parents and sisters; but, you can choose how you treat them. The best thing is to appreciate your parents, no matter what they look like. They gave you the precious gift of life, which no one else could. God chose them to bring you into this life. You cannot deny this fact or run away from it," Roselita explained bitterly. "I will never cease to be their mother and their stepmother will never give birth to them. Never."

Chebet remained quiet.

She heard the humming of a car behind the house.

"Who could that be?" she wondered. She then heard loud voices of children.

"They have come. The naughty children have come," Roselita commented while rising from her seat. Chebet did not know what to do.

The kitchen door was then opened forcibly.

"Who is this, Auntie?" The tall chocolate boy asked sarcastically. Roselita did not answer.

"I was asked to inform you that you need to do your homework after you take your tea," Roselita responded.

Another boy, followed by a girl, entered the kitchen. The girl slapped the boy before disappearing into the other door.

"Mum took away my phone yesterday but she isn't wise. We have the computer and a modem," the eldest boy said to no one in particular.

He then disappeared into the sitting room.

"One day you will start a family my dear; never forget that your presence will mean a lot to the children. Do not be so busy."

Chebet nodded not knowing how to react.

"You are a very bright girl. When I look at you, I know you have a good future," she continued as she lit what Chebet learnt was a gas cooker.

"When you grow rich and have children, please remember to create time for them. It will mean a lot. I tried to do this to my children but there was inadequate time. Their father ensured we separated. What I am saying is that a parent's presence really means a lot to children. These three children are really spoilt. Their parents are so busy that they do not have time for them. What has happened? The children are deformed in character and they can do and say anything. My daughter, never ever forget that. You may forget me, but please never forget my advice," she paused. "I was denied time to spend with my children when my husband took all of them to a boarding school at a very young age. I was then taken to his rural home."

"I will never forget you and your advice. You did not know me before but you treated me so well yesterday. I feel indebted to you."

"Thank you, daughter," she patted her shoulders as she looked for a cooking pan.

The second born came a few minutes later, a phone in his hands. Chebet did not know what it was at first because it was very broad. She was, however, told that it was called a Blackberry phone.

"Have you joined Facebook, Auntie?"

Roselita looked at the twelve-year old, Jeff.

"What is that?" she asked. Chebet was uneasy.

"This world must be very different. How could I ever come to compete with such people, when they were so much ahead in life?" she thought quietly.

"I interact with my friends. I see videos and I talk to my mother and father too."

Chebet looked confused.

"This is my friend," Jeff showed them the photo of the elderly woman on the phone. She was dressed in a white camisole and tight jeans. Her face was that of a teenager. Jeff moved closer to Chebet, something that made her uncomfortable. She gave a plastic smile, even as Jeff busied himself with his phone.

"Will you be staying here?" he asked.

"No, she cannot stay here," Jean responded from the door. He wore a pair of shorts only, leaving his chest exposed. He was holding a shirt in his hands.

Chebet was embarrassed and did not respond. She actually did not belong to that class of people and she would not get any sleep if she was told to spend the night there.

"Take your tea and do your homework," Roselita told them.

"No one will help us with the homework. Joyce went and you cannot do it, Auntie. Did you go to school?" Jean asked.

"Your mother will be cross with you if she discovers that you have not done your homework," Roselita went on.

"She will not know. She comes home late and leaves very early. Does your friend here go to school?" Jeff asked.

"Yes. She is in Class Six," Roselita responded on her behalf. Chebet looked at her proudly but with fear. Jeff disappeared only to come later carrying some books with him.

"Do it for me!" he demanded.

Chebet took the books and fearfully opened them. Jeff pointed at the assignment. She looked at Roselita who approved.

She started to write the answers.

"You have very good handwriting," Jeff stood by her side. Jean moved closer.

"You will also do my assignment," Jean said.

Roselita looked at Chebet and smiled.

"You are really smart, my dear girl."
Chebet shied off.

She continued to write the assignment for Jeff. It was English, her favourite subject.

Chapter Seventeen

Soft music came from Roselita's small radio after the 9 PM news, which Roselita seemed very interested in. She commented on one of the items: Members of Parliament refusing to pay tax. They argued that their money was used to assist the poor in their constituencies. This did not impress Roselita who argued that paying tax is every Kenyan's responsibility, irrespective of how many poor people they were assisting. Chebet did not understand the whole concept, but she had listened as Roselita passionately talked about the issue. She had gone back to her duties after the news.

"When do you rest?" Chebet asked.

"I work all through; I hate being idle," she responded while rinsing the plates they had used at supper. Chebet looked at her and felt pity that Roselita was living alone, while her children lived with another woman whom the children called mother. They led posh lifestyles while their mother struggled in her single room in a place that Chebet came to learn was called Gachie.

"My dear, you really shocked me but made me very proud."

"Why?" Chebet asked.

"You are really bright. You come from a very remote area but the way you did the assignments for Jean and Jeff stunned me. You learnt in a public school and had to rely on the Red Cross feeding programme."

"Yes. We were 65 pupils in our class and at times the chairs were not enough. I loved school very much. I wish I could continue," Chebet commented.

"You still have an opportunity," Roselita answered. "Do not give up. Haven't you seen old people going back to school? There is the famous Kimani Maruge who has joined the Guinness Book of Records as the oldest pupil. With passion and zeal, then time is not an issue."

"I will not give up. My resolve to go to school will remain and it doesn't matter how long it takes. For now, I pray for my brothers to continue."

Roselita remained quiet for a while.

"I like your determination to go back to school. We shall try our best. You are a nice girl. Your friends liked you very much."

"Yes, but Jeff said that I have a village mind and that I will become a housegirl even if I pass exams. He has very bad pictures in his TV."

"It's called a computer not TV. They are all spoilt because their mother and father are never present for them."

"Do they sell beer in the house?" Chebet asked ignorantly

"Why?"

"Jeff showed me bottles of beer in a cabinet. He wanted to give me some but I refused."

"No, that is for their parents. They stock it in the house for themselves. I once found Jeff trying to open a bottle," Roselita commented.

Chebet remained quiet, marvelling at what she saw in the house. Many of the things she saw were unfamiliar, including a TV that showed someone in full. Roselita had allowed her to interact with Rosemary's children, though she knew that would cause trouble if the mother knew of it. Roselita had openly told Chebet about that and she fearfully interacted with them, very keen on any movement within the compound. However, by the time they left that place at 8.30 PM, none of the parents had come; they left the children on their own, though there was a guard at the gate. There were two small dogs around the home. Chebet had screamed when one of the dogs jumped at her and started licking her hands. Jeff and Jean laughed at her. It was Joy, the six-year old girl who assisted her by chasing the dog away. She learnt that the dog was called Stacy.

"You did not tell me what you will do once you go home at the end of the month," Roselita asked, wiping her hands on her clothes before sitting on the bed. Chebet noticed that Roselita must have had a dimple when she was young and must have been beautiful. She had strands of grey hair on her head.

"I will go to work in the quarry," she responded briskly.

Roselita looked at her with pity.

"You cannot work in a quarry, my girl," she shook her head in disapproval.

"I worked there once. If I cannot work there, then I don't know."

"You told me your brothers are now with your uncle?"

"Yes, but I'm sure they will not continue staying there. My uncle is very bad. He will mistreat them. My mother told me that he would handle everything but..." she paused, "I don't trust him at all."

"What will happen if I fail to take my mother's advice? I am worried. Will I get a curse?" Chebet asked worriedly.

"No. You cannot get a curse for failing to abide by what someone said when she or he was alive and the words were evil or against God's will. God can never punish you for that," she consoled her. Chebet looked relived and gazed blankly at the stained iron sheet roofs.

"I will have to go home and take care of my brothers. They are so young and no one will take care of them."

"What about the neighbours and relatives?"

"They won't. People are so poor at our place. There is no food for visitors. I did not tell you that my mother used to live on the school food. We always hid food from school. We did not have anything to eat during the weekends unless the government gave the little food they used to give."

"What?"

"Yes. We used to carry food from school and take to her. You see, my father died and he was the one who used to provide. When my mother fell sick, there was no one else to get us food."

Roselita gave Chebet an incredulous look.

"I'm sorry about that. You have a story to tell," she commented. "Anyway, let's sleep. It's very late; I have to wake up very early tomorrow."

A phone call interrupted their discussion.

"I told them to sleep once I gave them supper," Chebet heard Roselita say. Chebet knew immediately that the call had come from Jean's mother.

"Okay… Okay… Yes." Roselita responded fearfully. "I will do that… Okay."

"We shall go together tomorrow. We shall wake up at 3.30am so that we can be there at 4.30am," she responded after the call.

"Is there a problem?" Chebet asked out of concern. She had noticed the change of mood in Roselita.

"Not really. You know she is drunk and has found her children watching a movie. I pity them. Money they have, yes, but their life is miserable."

"Do women drink alcohol?"

"My dear, the modern woman wants to be equal to man. You will one day understand. Today's women want to go out and drink with friends. They want to smoke. They want to remain out at night and have their fun. All these they want to do. Unfortunately, they fail to understand that the effect of all these is twice as much on them as on men. Men do not become pregnant. When they drink and smoke, the effect to their children is mostly psychological. When women do that, the effect on their children is more than psychological; it can be biological and physical. When you drink and smoke as a woman, you affect your reproductive organs. The modern woman does not realise that as she wants to be a man. Never do that, my dear."

"I will never do that," Chebet responded.

"What will make you stand upright and be respected is how you will treat and honour your womanhood. Respect it and do not even allow boys to play around with your body. You see, my girl, you are now maturing and can get pregnant. When you get pregnant, you interrupt so many things you were supposed to do. Boys will proceed and will, therefore, leave you behind. Take great care and look where you are going. Never forget this my girl, okay?"

"Okay," Chebet responded shyly.

She pulled down the curtain.

After a short while, she asked Chebet to join her in bed.

"I will get you a dress and some panties," Roselita commented, stretching on the bed. She pulled the blanket to cover herself. She put out the lamp after Chebet lay next to her on the bed and covered herself with the light blanket.

"There is so much that pupils and students need to know about life and themselves. I wish I can have the opportunity to educate young girls and boys about life. Then when I grow up, I will educate parents," Chebet thought as she drifted to sleep.

Chapter Eighteen

A number of weeks had gone by since Chebet came to Nairobi. At times she was excited to be in Nairobi and wished she could get the job of a housegirl. Life was different compared with Marigat so much so that she wondered if her dry but beautiful small town with all its livestock was even part of Kenya. She was pleasantly surprised to find that the books that Jeff, Jean and Joy were using in school were the same as the ones she used in her Marigat school. Though she noted that the three were very fluent in English, she was excited that she could beat them when it came to writing and answering questions from the textbooks. They had a great dislike for books and kept on bringing their assignments to Chebet to do. Their mother did not know this was happening but Chebet was terrified at the thought of Rosemary finding out.

There were days, however, when Chebet wished she were in Marigat, far away from the senseless city. She missed her brothers and school. On such nights, she sobbed quietly and made every effort to conceal her misery from Roselita.

Saturday night was the culmination of these bad days. She feigned a tummy ache and retreated to the toilet to weep. She worried about what could have become of her brothers. There was no one to tell her about them. When Roselita realised she had stayed for long in the toilet, she went for her. Roselita noted that she was crying.

"You don't have to keep on crying, my girl."

Roselita consoled Chebet when she opened the door of the toilet. Chebet's cheeks were moist with tears.

Chebet had broken a set of plates at Rosemary's house. As fate would have it, the plates came crashing down with a thunderous report just as Rosemary was getting off an emotive phone call with her contractors. The noise brought her running to the kitchen, her phone in one hand and a pen in the other. A wounded tigress would not have been angrier.

Rosemary launched into a torrent of expletives that left Chebet speechless.

"You clumsy, pea-brained, pathetic mistake of a girl! How dare you break my plates? Do you know how much they cost me to import them? Do you?" she bellowed.

No amount of apology and pleading would cool her down. She went on and on for ten straight minutes but to Chebet, it could as well have been a leap year of name calling, humiliation and berating that ended in her being dismissed without pay.

"Leave my house now!" Rosemary roared. "I never want to see you. Ever!!!" she thundered. "Leave!!!"

Rosemary continued to rant and rave long after a frightened Chebet had left. Were it not for her oversize dress, everyone would have noticed her shaking body.

When Rosemary finally cooled down, she summoned Roselita and announced she would not pay Chebet a penny. For good measure, the added, Roselita would have to take half-pay for not training her to handle Rosemary's cutlery with utmost care.

This was unfair and Rosemary knew as much but she did not care; she wanted someone or something to take out her frustrations on. What a perfect opportunity.

Chebet was traumatised and kept on crying whenever that incident cropped up in her mind. Though Jeff, Jean and Joy tried to persuade her to stay saying her mother had spoken in anger, Chebet resolved to go back to Marigat. No one had ever made such noise at her. She preferred a thorough beating to a minute of the humiliation and insults she received at the hands of Rosemary that fateful day. The little that remained of her self-esteem was shattered. She wondered why God had to allow such things to happen. Fine, the plates were imported, expensive and one of a kind but she did not break them intentionally.

She felt for Roselita who was also shouted at shamelessly. Roselita humbled herself even as she was insulted. Chebet had felt like telling Rosemary to stop insulting Roselita since she was not responsible for the breakages. She felt responsible for it all. When Roselita told her that there was no problem, Chebet did not believe her. She had let down Roselita, she told herself.

"My only fear is losing the job. Life is very hard here in Nairobi," she had said, making Chebet feel even more guilty and regret having come to Nairobi.

"I'm really sorry. I am responsible and regret every bit," Chebet had apologised profusely wishing she could talk to Rosemary and tell her not to dismiss Roselita.

"I'm going home tomorrow," she had finally told Roselita when they got to the house last night. She did not care whether she had the fare. Roselita had not commented, something that made Chebet boil with remorse.

The morning breeze was easing while birds hopped from one tree to the next as if celebrating the Sunday. They chirped one after another, apparently in a serious chit-chat, or singing. Maybe they were backbiting Chebet who sat at the door of the house. Roselita had gone to the shop to buy breakfast. She had not said anything about getting Chebet fare home or even escorting her to the bus station. She could not go to town on her own since she did not know where she was in terms of direction. She did not have the fare. But going home was her only option, as Rosemary had sworn to have her arrested on sight. Her daughter had shed tears on that, but she did not take back her words. She, therefore, could not go to that home. She did not see herself staying in Roselita's house the whole day doing nothing. Again, Roselita seemed unhappy with what had happened at Rosemary's house.

She stared at the beautiful bird hopping on the ground. She stared at it without blinking, though her mind was far away in a different world. She recalled the last time she was in class. It was the day she lost her mother.

"Will I ever go to school again?" she muttered.

She crossed her legs and fought back tears. It was her dream to get to Class Eight, where she had vowed to pass with flying colours so that she could get someone to sponsor her for secondary school education. Though she never went to church, this was the dream she prayed and lived for. Her father used to encourage her to pursue her dreams.

"What will happen to me now?" she asked softly.

Roselita came back carrying milk and bread in a black polythene bag.

"Please prepare yourself. We are going to church," she said.

Chebet rose indolently.

"Which church?" she asked.

"My church, St Teresa Catholic Church," she commented as she entered the house, Chebet following her.

"When will I go to my home?"

"You will not go home, my girl," Roselita faltered. "I talked to my friend and there is someone who needs a househelp. She will take you there so that you may negotiate the terms."

Chebet was confused. She did not know what to say.

"Is it a job?" she asked excitedly.

"Yes, it's a job. But I was informed that the woman is very strict; you will have to be very careful."

"I will be careful not to break plates and cups," she responded cautiously and full of remorse.

"We shall first go to church, then my friend will come for you in the afternoon. I know the pay is very bad but…"

"I do not care," she intercepted, "I just want to get something to do. Then I will take some money to my brothers. I will buy them clothes and food they have never eaten."

"That's fine," Roselita responded as she lit the paraffin stove. "But I'm keen on you getting back to school. Whatever we are doing is only a short-term measure. Take a bath. We shall attend the second mass, which starts at 10 AM."

"I have never gone to a Catholic church."

"No problem. This will be your first time." Roselita responded.

Chebet took a basin from under the bed and went to fetch water from the tap. There was a queue at the tap. She was too excited to worry about the queue. She fell in line with a huge smile on her face. She did not just have a chance at a new job but Roselita had forgiven her. God sure works in a mysterious way, she mused. A few minutes ago she was all set to travel back home, fare or none, but now she was more than ready to take a new job – even if the pay was as bad as Roselita made it sound.

She will wear the secondhand dress that Roselita bought her.

Chapter Nineteen

Roselita entered through what appeared to be the main door of the big and spacious church. She touched a small basin of water that was attached to the wall at the entrance, then bowed. She made a sign of the cross. Chebet was confused and did not know what to do. Some activities and actions followed so fast that she lost track. She just followed Roselita to the front seat, where they sat a pew behind the group of uniformed members. The uniformed people sang in different voices and danced joyfully to the song. The front and second rows had women only, while the third had both men and women. The fourth and fifth rows had men only. A man was playing piano at the side.

Roselita knelt and closed her eyes. She started to pray. Chebet followed suit. She knelt but her eyes remained open. She studied the beautiful church with so much curiosity.

The church was in the shape of a cross, with doors at every corner. The floor was tiled. The aisle had tiles of a different texture and colour. It led to the raised altar, where a table covered with immaculate and beautifully decorated and laced cotton material took the pride of place. A dim light flickered behind the three seats next to the altar. Chebet had never seen such a beautiful church and she felt like she was seeing God. The statue of the mother holding a child in her hands reminded her of her mother. She closed her eyes unconsciously.

"Mother, you are watching me. Please guide us your children," she prayed.

She sat on the pew and watched the smartly dressed people enter the church, bow and occupy various positions. A group of children, guided by an elderly woman, entered through a side door and occupied four pews just a few metres from the door. The children looked disciplined and were respectfully quiet. They were of different ages with the eldest being her age. Some of them knelt and prayed earnestly.

Chebet clapped her hands but not in rhythm to the song that Roselita sang so fluently.

Everyone stood up; a few turned their eyes to the last pew. From where she stood, Chebet could not see. However, she realised that the priest was matching to the altar, led by dancing girls in uniform. Chebet admired the way they were dancing. The priest, in a green robe, blessed people by sprinkling holy water on them. The people responded by making a sign of the cross.

The priest, accompanied by three boys in white robes, went behind the altar. They wore similar dresses to the ones her mother had worn in her dream.

When the song ended, the priest started with a sign of the cross; everybody else did the same.

"Brothers and sisters, we congregate here on this twenty-first Sunday of the year. Our readings today focuses on prayer. The question is: What do you want God to do for you? Have you prayed to Him confidently? What do you want Him to do for you today?" he continued.

"I want to go to school. I want my brothers to continue with school too," Chebet said quietly.

She followed the mass with enthusiasm, attempting all the gestures that included standing and sitting. When it came to the sermon, Chebet noticed that the children who had come as a group, belonged to a children's home located a short distance from the church. The priest invited them to perform a skit titled "Prayers." Chebet was moved by the performance, which she found lively.

After the skit and as one of the girls explained the story behind the skit, Chebet noticed Roselita stealing worried glances at her. The woman to the left of Chebet was shaking her head in what appeared to be sorrow and disbelief. She had a hand to her lips while a thin film of tears lined her eyes.

"Who takes care of them?" Chebet whispered to Roselita.

"We shall talk later," Roselita said, not taking her eyes off the priest who was now talking about the role of parents in bringing up their children in the way of the Lord.

"These children are orphans. Some were abandoned by their parents. What is happening dear parents? How can you bring an innocent person to this world, only to expose them to suffering? Why would you do that?" the priest asked.

This was one topic Chebet found easy to follow for she could easily identify with the pains and woes of orphans. She was an orphan and the short time she had lived as one was not one she was in a hurry to relive. It was like a nightmare she could not wait to wake up from. Her mind was in a million different places playing catch-up to her thoughts. Not Marigat, not her two brothers, not her emaciated mother lying in bed waiting for her death, not her former school, not Rosemary with her expensive chinaware, not the three Js (for that is what she called Rosemary's children), not Roselita's humble abode, not her oversize dress, not her ambitions, not her next job (it may have been a housegirl's job but to her, it might as well been the IMF director's job), not … Let us just say her mind was everywhere and nowhere. The sight of the orphans awakened something in her that left her restless and set her mind wandering.

"What if everyone knows my story?" she thought. "My parents were good but fate took them away."

While Chebet was lost in the maze of her thoughts, the mass came to an end. It jerked her back to the present. The whole church stood up as one and bowed their heads for closing prayers.

"So many children are suffering. Why does God allow this?" Chebet asked after one of the children said a very emotive prayer of how children have been psychologically and physically abandoned by their parents and left to the uncaring eyes of the world. Though the boy read the prayer from a paper, it was so emotional that Chebet noticed the woman next to her shed a tear.

"Does this happen always? Do these children come to this church always? How does one get to join the children's home?" she asked herself.

The mass ended after two hours. People matched out of the church slowly. Roselita and Chebet stayed behind for a short while. As Chebet observed the children go out one by one, Roselita knelt and said a short prayer. By the time she was done, there was hardly anyone at the door.

"Let's see someone for a short while. Please follow me," Roselita instructed her after talking to some women.

Chebet followed her towards the priest's house. At the door, Roselita pressed the bell, which was answered by a young man.

"I want to see Father Joachim," Roselita said. Chebet's eyes and mind were on the compound. She took a keen interest in the white cat that basked lazily in the sun, a few metres from the door.

Father Joachim appeared shortly.

"Christ the Kingdom come, Father?" Roselita extended her hand joyfully to the priest. Chebet did the same and was excited when the priest held her and drew her close.

They talked a little more about some small Christian community, before Roselita introduced Chebet.

"Father, this is Milcah Chebet, the little girl I told you about," Roselita began.

"Oh, this is the courageous orphan who preferred a strange city to early marriage? How are you my daughter?" Father Joachim began, still holding a very shy Chebet.

"I am fine, Father. I am happy to meet you," Chebet answered.

The priest then ushered them into the house.

Ever a rural girl, all Chebet noticed when they entered the house were the comfortable seats and a flask of tea. The sweet aroma of mandazi and roasted groundnuts did not escape her sharp sense of smell. She surrendered to the little pleasures but just for a while.

"Take a seat, take a seat," the priest directed them.

Chebet sat close to Roselita. She looked like she would disappear into Roselita's dress at a moment's notice. Such was her fear.

Father Joachim offered them tea, mandazi and groundnuts before they got down to discussing Chebet's case. Roselita started to update the priest but he motioned her to stop.

"Let me hear you tell your story, my daughter," he told Chebet, "Go on."

Chebet looked at Roselita who nodded for her to proceed. She was still not sure how to go about it. She breathed in and began her story. She started off nervously but gained confidence as she went on.

Once filled with confidence and her composure regained, Chebet delved into her story right from the death of her father and her mother's struggles to the famine, death of their livestock and her mother's sickness to her mother's death. She had to pause a few times to catch her breath or wipe away a tear and steady her voice. When she got to the day her mother was buried and their moving to her uncle's home, it was too much to bear but Roselita urged her on.

She told the priest about the arranged marriage, how she went back to their home with her siblings and sought work at the quarry before finally escaping to Nairobi. Her tribulation on getting to Nairobi all the way to being hired by Rosemary was too much for Father Joachim to bear. For the first time in her life, Chebet saw a grown-up man weep. She was shocked.

Her narration was clear so no one asked for clarification or for her to repeat anything. In conclusion, she acknowledged Roselita's saving role in her life. She expressed her desire to continue with her education and return home to change Marigat.

"That would be my wish," she concluded.

Father Joachim excused himself and walked out to answer a call on his cellphone.

"I'm impressed, my daughter. That was very good and Father Joachim was moved. He will do something for you and your brothers," Roselita told her.

"Will my brothers and I go to school now?" she asked.

Roselita nodded in agreement. Chebet looked up at the ceiling and smiled.

"I cannot believe this. If I go to school, I will study very hard. I will then assist children from Marigat, especially girls. They are forced into circumcision then married off at my age."

"Yes, you told me," Roselita reminded her. "I know you have a good heart and will do that. Your mother and father will be smiling wherever they are."

They heard Father Joachim approach while talking over the phone. He stopped at the door and gestured as he talked. Chebet saw a big scar he had at the back of his head.

"Sorry for leaving you two to yourselves but I am back," he said as he settled into the seat across Chebet and Roselita.

He spoke about Chebet's admirable courage and unrelenting spirit. He told her he was impressed and would continue to pray for her and her siblings.

"I have spoken to three children's homes and sent members of the church to three others. We are looking for a home that can accommodate you and your siblings," he said.

Chebet could not believe what she had heard but concealed her excitement; she reserved for the time they would be back at Roselita's.

A short while later, the priest saw them off and promised to visit them later.

✵✵✵✵✵

Three weeks later, the priest sent for Roselita and Chebet.

"I have talked to the owner of Mother of Hope Children's Home," he told them as soon as they were seated.

"She has agreed to admit you and your two brothers at her institution."

"What?" Chebet exclaimed.

She thought she was dreaming. She gave in to her emotions and fell at the priest's feet, weeping. She was overwhelmed with joy.

The best was yet to come.

"I will also admit you to St Claire Primary School, where the three of you will attend class paid for by the parish. You will be under me, though you will also belong to this parish, as children of this parish. St Claire belongs to the church, while the children's home is under the care of one of our committed members."

"Thank you so much! Thank you. I want my brothers to know…"

"I will drive you to your home. We shall go pick them there."

Chebet could not believe it. She gazed at Roselita through her tears. Roselita was in tears too.

"I'm very glad, Mum," she said, shaking her head in disbelief.

"Father, thank you so much; God bless you abundantly," Roselita went on.

"I will never let you down," Chebet promised no one in particular.

"It's okay, my daughter," Father Joachim responded, the gap in his upper teeth becoming manifest. "Roselita will bring you here tomorrow."

"I will not manage to bring her but I will get someone to do that, Father."

Chebet was lost for words. She stared at him, wondering what she would do to thank him and Roselita. She felt like rolling on the tiled floor with excitement.

Nothing mattered more than the opportunity to go back to school.

Chapter Twenty

The chirping of insects and the whining of motor vehicles were the common noises she heard throughout the night. There was some soft wind that occasionally ruffled the leaves of the trees in the compound. Two drunkards passing by the house intercepted her thoughts. She listened as they talked while drifting to their homes. She experienced the changes in weather and covered herself well when the dawn chill approached and made the water that had condensed on the iron-sheet roof start to drip. She longed for the day and its light to come and displace the darkness and cold that defined the night. Almost an hour had gone by since Roselita left for Rosemary's house, where she was to prepare the children for school. Chebet wished for a chance to talk to Jeff, Jean and Joy to tell them that she was going to Marigat.

"I will pass your regards," Roselita had responded when Chebet made the request.

"I'm very happy and proud of you, my girl. In the few days we have stayed together, you have made me feel like a mother," Roselita talked emotionally. "I'm so happy that I will contribute to a change in your life and have you and your brothers back in school. This is great to me and I feel fulfilled. I urge you to make use of the opportunity. Give it your best, my daughter."

"I will, Auntie," Chebet responded.

"You are really bright, Chebet. I pray that you never lose that focus. You do not have your parents, but if you so wish, I will be there as your mother, whenever you need me. I will be there for you and I look forward to seeing your siblings in the evening."

"Thank you, Auntie," Chebet answered in tears.

"You have taken care of me and have ensured that I get back to school. You will not regret doing this; I will pray for you every day and ask God to bless you."

"I will meet you at Mother of Hope in the evening. Remember that though you will be staying there, I will be here for you and your brothers. I will visit you frequently and will ask Aunt Sabella to allow you to visit me every Sunday."

"Thank you so much. You bought me clothes and..."

"No, no, no, please! Nothing to thank me for. I will see you in the evening. When you lock the house, please carry the key with you. I have a spare key."

"Thank you," Chebet concluded before Roselita left the house. She wept at the thought of Roselita not accompanying them. She would have wished for Roselita to see her home in Marigat. Roselita was born in Murang'a, in Central Kenya and had never visited the Rift Valley.

Chebet had never come across such a good woman. Indeed the ethnicity mindset that her mother had imbued in her changed. Her mother hated the Kikuyu community and had made Chebet become suspicious of her Kikuyu friends. The head teacher only made the perception worse. She now did not harbour any ill feeling towards the Kikuyu community. She realised that a community is never bad, just individuals. Good and bad individuals are there in every community. It is wrong to base your judgement of a community on one or two people. Her mother had made that mistake. Had she followed her mother's ill-informed advice, she may have failed to notice or even enjoy Roselita's kindness. Roselita had led her to a new phase of her life. Chebet now loved her as a mother and was happy that she had a woman who stood in for her mother. This was a big achievement and she knew her brothers would love her too.

She rose from the bed and took a basin to the tap. She fetched enough water for her bath. Everything appeared to be happening like in a movie. She still could not believe it.

Roselita had bought her a blue pair of jeans, a white blouse, a pair of sandals and three camisoles. She advised her to be wearing camisoles since her breasts were growing bigger.

She wore the new dress with the white camisole. When she wore the sandals, the feeling that she was very smart overwhelmed her so much that she looked at herself in the mirror with so much pride. Roselita was spoiling her, even going as far as buying her lotion – a first in her life. She walked in style in the house, wishing her former classmates would see her on her return.

She picked some trousers that Roselita had bought Julius and Dennis. Roselita had argued that they needed to look smart while travelling to Nairobi. She had bought them a pair of trousers each, T-shirts and shoes. Though they were secondhand, the clothes looked good enough and Chebet knew that they would be very excited. Roselita had sacrificed a lot. Chebet noticed that she had used almost all her money on them. She did not know what to say, but she promised to give Roselita a treat of her life in future. She could build her a house, for starters.

She packed the clothes in Roselita's bag and put the money she had been given in the pocket. When she was done, she walked out of the house and waited impatiently for the priest who had promised to come for her at the house. Chebet did not want to sit down lest the clothes lose their new feel.

She stood at the door, a broad smile occasionally passing like a wave on her lips. The smile was brighter, especially when she heard the buzzing of a car and noticed that it was Father Joachim. He was driving a grey car, a RAV4 she learnt later. She dashed to the house and took the bag.

It was unbelievable that she would be driven home in a personal car. She wished her mother and father were there to witness but she recalled that had they been around, life would have been different. God works in a mysterious way, His wonders to perform, she told herself, echoing a phrase she last heard in Marigat.

She locked the house and walked to the car, a spring of pride in her strides.

Chapter Twenty-one

By 2 PM, Chebet and Father Joachim were at her home in Marigat. Excitement boiled inside her when they reached her former school. When she alighted from the car, she might as well have been walking on air. She felt so light. Pupils stared at them openly while the few teachers who dared overcome their curiosity, pretended not to see but Chebet could swear they were dying to hide behind some peep hole and stare at Chebet and Father Joachim all day long.

Chebet led Father Joachim to the head teacher's office, where they both entered and had a brief chat with the head teacher who after casually informing them that Chebet's brothers were not in school, went on to talk of the countless problems the school was facing. Chebet had lost interest in the conversation and was wondering why her brothers were not in school. As usual, the head teacher did not show much concern, his mind, going by the drift of his talk, was on getting some money or help from the priest.

Before they left the school, Chebet had excused herself for a few minutes to talk to her friend, Janet. She was so excited to see her and Chebet promised to always remember her and to one day come for her. She gave her a twenty-shilling coin, which excited

Janet very much. Kipchirchir had approached them as they talked but Chebet did not show the dislike she previously had for him.

Chebet and Father Joachim left for her home but on reaching the compound found no one. She looked around – the former cowshed, the bedrooms – but got no clue. However, when she got to the kitchen, she realised that they had cooked the previous day; the cooking pans were still dirty.

She got out and walked to where Father Joachim was standing.

"They are not here, Father," she said.

"Oh, where could they be, in the fields, perhaps?" he asked.

"I don't think so. Let's check at my uncle's home; a short distance from here," she answered.

Since the road to her uncle's home was rough, they left the car and walked there. To Chebet's surprise, Father Joachim managed the whole distance despite his being fat.

She saw her aunt from a distance, seated outside the house weaving a basket. When her aunt saw them, she rose from the block she was sitting on and stared at them, disbelief written all over her face. Chebet was very excited.

"This is my aunt," Chebet said to the priest.

"I am Father Joachim from Nairobi. I'm a friend of Chebet's and she has invited me to her home."

"Welcome Father, welcome. Let's go to the house. It's very hot here and I can see you are already sweating…"

"No, it's okay. I wouldn't want us to stay for long. We are going back to Nairobi."

Chebet's aunt seemed confused.

"You travelled to Nairobi Cheb?" she asked, trying to engage them.

"Yes and I will go to school there. I will not get married and I will not be circumcised. When I finish school, I will come back and mobilise the girls to say no to such practices," Chebet affirmed. Father Joachim smiled.

"I pray for you, Cheb," her aunt said with a shaking voice.

"Where are my brothers?" She finally asked.

"They ran away as soon as you left," she paused. "I don't know. Their uncle had said he would look for them today. He has gone for a meeting convened by the chief about cattle rustling. Livestock was stolen yesterday…"

Chebet was confused.

"Maybe they went to the quarry," Chebet thought aloud.

"Could be. We can go together to check on them."

They left the home, Chebet's aunt leading them. Father Joachim did not talk much. Chebet hoped he did not hate the place.

It took forty-five minutes to get to the quarry.

"Are those women working here?" Father Joachim asked.

"Yes. Women work here. Their husbands do nothing but look after livestock-for those with surviving livestock. Many women are left with no option but to work here and earn some money," Chebet's aunt responded. Father Joachim shook his head in disbelief.

"Even children?"

"Yes."

"This is unfair. We have a government that talks of meeting targets on their tax collection, yet people are suffering. This is very unfair. You have a member of parliament?"

"Yes, we do; but he never comes here. People are dying because of hunger here. We survive by the grace of the Lord often, through the assistance of Red Cross, which is like the government here," she commented.

Father Joachim was shocked to see children crushing stones. He drew closer to the children, bringing the whole quarry to a stop. The women working in the quarry, some with babies strapped on their backs, also stopped working to find out what the priest wanted in their humble place of work.

"These are my brothers," Chebet said, introducing two boys who were covered in white dust. She held them close not caring about the dust. Father Joachim moved towards them and shook their hands. They were initially hesitant but they finally shook hands with the priest.

"Are they not supposed to be in school?" Father Joachim asked.

"Yes..." Chebet's aunt responded.

"They have to make some money. We are alone and..."

A group of men, women and children who all looked very emaciated, probably because of the demanding work at the quarry, stood around Chebet and Father Joachim.

Something awoke inside Chebet and gave her courage she did not know she had and before she could tell what was happening, she started addressing the crowd.

"Sorry for interrupting your work," she started, "I have come with a visitor from Nairobi. He is Father Joachim. He is here to pick up my brothers and take us to school."

She looked at Father Joachim and said, "This is where I come from and this is our life here. This is all the work we have. Were it not for the Red Cross, there would be many more children here, preferring work to school. Life here is hard but we do all we can to stay alive."

Dennis and Julius looked surprised.

"I am Father Joachim from Nairobi as the brave girl has said. I met her in Nairobi and heard her story of struggle, sorrow and destitution. The church will sponsor her and her brothers. We are here to take them with us."

They left after a few minutes. Father Joachim, Chebet, her brothers and her aunt.

"Cheb, Uncle chased us from his home. He said we are useless," Dennis told her when they were a few metres from the aunt, "We went to our home…" Father Joachim looked at Dennis.

"Are we going with you Cheb? Please do not leave us here. We are so hungry; we had very little food yesterday."

"We shall go together, little boy. You will stay with her. You will also go to a very good school," Father Joachim commented.

They continued talking as they walked to their home.

"Cheb, shall we be carried by this car?" Julius asked, running his hands over the side of the vehicle parked in their homestead.

By four o'clock, they were packed and ready to go. The boys could not stop smiling, what with the clothes and shoes Cheb had brought, which they now wore.

"Excuse me for a moment, I need to do something," she said as she walked towards her mother's grave.

"Mum, I thank you for everything you did and said to me. I'm going to start another life, which I believe you would be pleased with. I miss you, Mum. I know you are fine wherever you are and you are not suffering anymore. I'm sorry I never lived up to your words…" she heard footsteps behind her and stopped.

Father Joachim had followed her to the graveside but remained a short distance behind, perhaps trying not to disturb Chebet's quiet moment.

Chebet rose from the ground, tears trickling down her cheeks.

"Is this where your mother was buried?"

"Yes."

He bowed down his head, made the sign of the cross and said a short prayer.

"I bless you in the name of the Father and of the Son and the Holy Spirit, amen," he muttered while making the sign of the cross.

They walked back to the car and boarded it. Father Joachim got out some money and gave Chebet's aunt who stood beside the car, tears in her eyes.

"I'm very grateful, Father. You do not know how I feel for these children. I did not have an option, but I quietly prayed for them. I'm so happy that they will get back to school and..." she shed a tear. "... I was not for the idea of her getting married but..."

"It's okay," Father Joachim responded. "I'm very glad also. I know I have taken these children without following the due process, but sometimes, due process gets in the way. I will talk to the local parish priest to follow up with the administration and Chebet's uncle. I promise that I will take care of them."

"You are too kind, Father. Thank you so much," she said bowing her head as if inviting the priest to lay his hand on her head to bless her.

"God bless you," he concluded as he started the car.

Chebet stared at her home with sorrow. She waved continuously at her aunt. Their life was changing fast.

"Shall we be staying in Nairobi?" Julius asked her. She shook her head. He then muttered something to his brother.

"When I grow up, I will buy a car like this one" Chebet heard Julius mumble to Dennis. She smiled at that. They could dare dream now.

"When I grow up, I want to be an ambassador for the marginalised areas and people. I would like to assist the people of Marigat and ensure they go to school and stop retrogressive cultural beliefs," Chebet said thoughtfully.

"That is very good. You will be the best ambassador to these people." Father Joachim told her.

Chebet nodded.

She gazed at the dry hills that faced the small town, where they used to go for shopping. The land was bare and only a few trees were visible. Though the sun was setting, it was hot enough to make Father Joachim sweat profusely.

She raised her hand and waved to the trees unknowingly. She rejoiced quietly that she made the best choice by risking going to the city. Life was changing for her siblings. She vowed to change life in her community and to be a role model.

"When you grow up, what will you become?" she recalled the question by the woman who had visited them at their school. She started to think about it once again.

Chapter Twenty-two

Father Joachim parked the car next to a tree. Security lights illuminated the beautifully tiled administration block. An elderly woman in a veil approached them and shook hands with the priest first, then each of them. Dennis and Julius stood on either side of Chebet, with Julius studying the place with so much curiosity. The lights at the entry of the offices seemed to have arrested his attention. He gestured to Dennis who was equally lost in a scene of children running after each other on the verandah. He smiled broadly. Chebet, too, was taking in the sights before her as she extended her hand to greet the lady, introduced to them as Sister Nelly. Father Joachim said that she was the head teacher of St Claire Primary School. She appeared jovial, a trait that drove Chebet to love her instantly, longing to start her classes. She was promised that they would start their class the following day, a breach in the protocol in their admission notwithstanding.

"I know we ought to have involved your family in this, but we shall go on," Father Joachim said.

"There is no problem, Father. In case of anything, I'm sure Roselita will stand in for my family," she answered.

Unknown to her, Roselita was in the same compound, walking towards them. Chebet ran to her and hugged her.

"Auntie, I missed you. Come, see my brothers."

"Thank you, my girl. Greet my friends first."

She shook hands with two women who had accompanied Roselita, but she did not let go of Roselita's hand.

"My brothers are so happy," Chebet enthused as they approached her brothers.

"How are you, Sabella?" Father Joachim saluted her.

"You managed..." she started to speak.

"Yes, I did... but I'm telling you, it is a journey and a half. The life there! Oh my God!"

"I know what you mean, Father. Oh, these are my sons? How are you? What are your names?" Sabella asked joyfully.

"He is Julius and this one is Dennis, our last born," Chebet introduced them excitedly.

"Oh, my good Dennis, I'm Aunt Sabella," she tickled him, much to his delight. Dennis stood there twiddling his thumbs shyly.

"Welcome so much..." Roselita said. Chebet held on to her dress excitedly. "This will be your home... Sister Nelly will be your teacher. A bus will pick you up in the morning. Aunt Sabella will take care of you here at the home. Chebet, remember our promise?" she paused.

"I will be visiting you but Aunt Sabella will let you visit me on Sundays, when you wish."

Chebet felt like weeping.

"I'm grateful to Father Joachim for his willingness to…"

"No, no, no! You do not have to thank me, please," Father Joachim reiterated. Roselita did not stop.

"I also thank Sister Nelly and Aunt Sabella for accepting these children. She was brought in by my boss to work only for her to be chased away soon after. I took care of her like I would my own daughter. She is a good girl…" she paused.

"On their behalf, I am grateful for your willingness," she stopped, gratitude overcoming her and leaving her in tears.

Chebet wanted to say something but Father Joachim intercepted. Aunt Sabella disappeared when Father Joachim started talking.

A group of children appeared just as Father Joachim finished speaking. Julius whispered something to Chebet, but she did not hear as her attention had drifted to the children, some much younger than her youngest brother. The children started singing a welcome song and dancing. They moved towards them and in a minute, the children had surrounded them with dance and song. Chebet was amazed.

She forgot how tired she was and joined them in the dance. The words of the song were so strong, welcoming them to a community of children who looked forward to the future with hope; never into a past that would never help. The girl who led the song and dance was so jovial to the extent she infected Chebet with her gaiety.

What a wonderful home, she thought, as she danced along. Roselita and Sabella had joined in the song and dance.

Chebet felt an excitement she had never felt. She and her brothers now belonged to the Community of Mary Mother of Hope Children's Home. Life was changing drastically.

Chapter Twenty-three

She knelt on the pew and closed her eyes to pray. Julius sat a few metres away while Dennis was two pews behind, sitting with his new friends with whom they went to school together. It had been exactly two months ago, when she first visited the church in the company of Roselita. The visit transformed her life. She now had a community, which she belonged to and had gone back to class, where she emerged the best in the end of term exams. Her popularity had grown both at the home and school. She was also a friend to every child in the home and was assigned the task of taking care of the young ones in the home. She enjoyed the task and felt very good and fulfilled. Her brothers were also disciplined and they, too, were given varied responsibilities.

She thanked God for all the blessings, before she rose and sat on the pew, next to two children aged four and five who were under her care.

Roselita walked in and occupied the same seat they occupied the first day she came to the church. Roselita smiled broadly and waved at Chebet before she knelt on the pew and prayed. She was a prayerful woman and kept on urging Chebet and her siblings to always pray. They met every Sunday after mass and proceeded to

Roselita's house to be back in the home by six o'clock. She had become a mother to them and was concerned about their well-being. Chebet longed for the mass to end so that she could join Roselita. She was grateful for what she constantly did for them and Chebet never forgot to pray for her. She vowed to build a house for her when she grew up.

She winked at Grace, her friend and classmate. Grace occupied the front seat and was ready to lead in a choral verse that they had rehearsed and were to present after the service. The choral verse was titled "Parents" and was written by one of the caretakers at the home. They fondly referred to her as Nanny. She was talented in music and taught new songs time and again. Children loved her.

Chebet had, however, seen her carry home items that were brought in by visitors. This had made her feel bad, though she did not inform anyone. She learnt later that a majority of the people who worked at the home carried away the items that were brought by visitors; that is why they still had torn blankets and mattresses even when visitors brought them new ones. Grace who had been in the home since she was three, told her that the owners of the home were worried that if they gave them the new blankets, mattresses and clothes, visitors would get the impression that they were doing very well and would therefore not assist them. They had to appear desperate all the time so that anyone seeing them would be moved to contribute. Chebet felt this was wrong. The staff and owner of the home took advantage of the children's plight to enrich themselves. This, however, did not distract her from her focus: school and the good community of children she had. Whether they stole everything, it was none of her business.

She did not mind eating githeri a whole week, never mind that guests always brought maize flour and rice on Sunday. The good thing was that she and her siblings had a very caring mother who ensured that they remained smart and that they enjoyed living at the home. However, they always longed for Sunday, when they would visit Roselita and eat something different.

Grace walked to her. Since there was no space on the pew, she bent and started whispering in her ear.

"Cheb, you will assist me. Nanny wants us to lead the choral verse. You will take the microphone, okay? I have flu."

"Okay," Chebet responded, before Grace went back to her seat.

"I have seen auntie, Cheb," Julius whispered immediately Grace had left. He pointed at Roselita who noticed and waved back with a smile.

Chebet smiled again. Were it not for her, she did not know where she would be. May be she would be working at the quarry.

She looked back and waved to her brother, Dennis. They had not talked since morning and she had not commended him for coming first in exams with very high marks.

"Your family is very bright and intelligent. You were number one in our class and your brother was number one too. Nanny was telling me that I should learn English from you," Grace had told her.

Chebet had just smiled, not sure what to say. She, however, felt proud and promised herself to work even harder. Roselita never stopped encouraging them.

Father Joachim led the mass. Chebet was glad that she was the one to lead the choral verse in his presence. She longed for the service to end.

An hour and a half later, they were called to the front of the church. They walked in an orderly manner and stood in the shape of a curve, the small and short children taking the first row. Chebet and Grace stood at the end of the first row with Chebet holding the microphone. She introduced the verse and paused to wait for the clapping to die down before getting to the verse itself. She saw Roselita give a thumbs-up sign, while Nanny smiled proudly. Chebet was more than motivated to lead the choral verse if only to make Roselita proud. She threw herself into the choral verse and gave it her all.

After the verse, she led the children in their popular song, which referred to them as winners. Though they had not been told to perform another song, they sent the congregation to further heights of excitement with the song. The children sang their hearts out and when they were done, the whole church burst into applause. Nanny looked so happy.

"That was great, my girl. I'm so happy."

"Thank you," Chebet said, as she tapped Grace on the shoulders. Loud murmurs filled the whole church, all eyes glued on Chebet. Roselita gave Chebet yet another thumbs-up sign, this time with both hands. Chebet did not know how to react; she just wiped sweat off her face.

A beaming Father Joachim took the microphone from her and after some silence, started talking.

"Unbelievable! I tell you, unbelievable! Chebet, come here and greet these good people…" He faced the children. Chebet rose and boldly matched towards the altar. The congregation burst into applause again.

"This girl is unique. She is unbelievable. I took her from her home in Marigat. She lost both her parents and was forced to work in the quarry to take care of her siblings. Her brothers, younger than her, joined in working at the quarry. I was impressed by her determination to live and the will to succeed… Please tell them who you are my dear and why you are here at Mother of Hope Children's Home."

Chebet waited patiently for the clapping to die down.

When she started speaking, the church went dead quiet. She was bold and spoke with authority and clarity. Her voice had that arresting quality that kept the listeners hanging on her every word as she told the story of her life.

Chapter Twenty-four

C hebet lifted the doll that she was given when she addressed the whole church two months ago. She knew she gave it her best shot. She could tell from their reaction that they were moved by her story. By the time she was done with the speaking, many in the congregation were dumbfounded. They rushed to shake her hand as they walked out of the church. They congratulated and encouraged her.

She read the card for the hundredth time:

"I have suffered for a couple of years with diabetes. My suffering had reached an end and I had given up. But when I heard your story today, all that changed. I hated myself for losing hope and becoming a loser as you said. Your words, however, transformed me and since then, I have gained the hope to live. I have realised there are better things ahead, just like you have a bright future ahead for never giving up. Your determination will uplift people. True to your words, young talented girl, every dark dawn has a morning.

Chebet, you will forever remain a role model to me and my family.

Thank you so much and may you continue to encourage people in this life full of hurdles."

She closed the card and put the doll away as Grace entered the hall. Chebet had come to the study hall after the nine o'clock news to do some writing.

"Last year we won in the music festival with a folk dance. We were dancing like this…" she demonstrated. "The music teacher said that we shall do another Luyia dance," Grace went on.

"He told me I would represent the school with a poem. I used to recite poems in my former school," Chebet responded proudly, showing Grace the poem, "But it's long. I want to write a narrative instead."

"A narrative?"

"Yes, a narrative will tell a story. It's more interesting than this poem."

"How will you do that?" Grace asked as she occupied the seat next to her.

"I have already started."

Chebet showed her a paragraph of her writing. It was titled "Responsibility." Grace started to read.

"Did your parents do this?" Grace asked.

"My father would have done it but only if he had gone to school to the end. He was very brilliant and read every bit of writing he came across. I wish he were alive to witness this. I'm writing this for my parents."

"Your family is very brilliant. You, Julius and Dennis are very brilliant."

Chebet hunched her shoulders as if to shrug off the compliment.

"Is it good?" she asked.

"What? The narrative? It is wonderful. Are you going to present it alone?"

"Yes. I wish I could present with you. But it's not possible," Chebet answered. Just then, Bobby, a fourteen-year old boy joined them. He was in Class Seven and a good friend of Grace. He shook hands with them and patted Grace on the back in a way Chebet did not find comfortable.

"What are you doing in the study hall at this hour?" he asked.

Before either of the girls could respond, Ken, Bobby's friend, walked in wearing a pair of shorts and a T-shirt, despite the chilly evening. Chebet was in a long skirt and heavy woollen pullover. Grace was a know-it-all and wore tight, blue jeans. The silk blouse she wore underneath the sleeveless jacket revealed the curves of her relatively big breasts, which Bobby unashamedly stared at. Chebet did not like it at all.

Ken sat on the table next to them. He winked at Bobby.

"Cheb, you never want to socialise with us. I only see you with the babies, or with your brothers."

"I watch over them."

"Yeah, but you need, er, you know, er..." Bobby stammered under the harsh glare of Chebet.

"Grace has not told you that, er, Ken, wants, er, you know, Ken would like to be your friend," Bobby continued.

Chebet looked at Grace who was shaking her head as if to deny the report.

"There is nothing bad, Cheb," Grace started, trying to stretch a hand to touch Chebet. "You know that Bobby is my friend. Ken can be your friend…"

"We are not in the same class and I …" Chebet responded but Grace would not let her finish.

"It's not like that, Cheb," Ken moved closer to her and placed an arm across her shoulders. Chebet did not move but one could see she was getting angry. Ken touched her hand but Chebet tried to draw it away.

"Don't be naive. We want to train you how life is around here. We are adults."

"I'm sorry but I do not want your kind of friendship. I'm not an adult yet – I'm growing to be one."

She grabbed her books to leave but Ken grabbed her and tried to kiss her. Bobby was kissing Grace who did not seem to mind; her eyes were closed in a way to show she was happy about it.

"Try it out Cheb. It is so sweet," Grace, breathless but still in Bobby's embrace implored her.

Ken made another attempt at bringing his lips closer to Chebet's but she pushed him away.

"Don't touch me or I will scream. I will tell Nanny of what you are doing," she shouted, making them stop whatever they were doing.

She then walked to the door.

"I know what I want in life and I don't need such friends to help me get there. You are all lost."

She then disappeared into the corridor and matched to the dormitories.

"When you are a teenager, you are yet to mature, but you are maturing. Leave the body to mature without interrupting it. Concentrate on your education and avoid anything that distracts you from your goals," she recalled Roselita's words uttered a few days ago.

"Something can stop you from achieving your goals. Somebody can stop you from achieving the goals. But you have the choice to stop something or somebody from doing that."

She stopped at the corridor and looked back. Grace, Bobby and Ken were leaving the hall too.

"I have to complete this narrative," she resolved, "No one should stop me from doing this."

She walked back to the hall and passed the three on the corridor. Bobby whispered "naive" when she got within touching distance but Chebet ignored him.

"Grace, you have your life and I have mine. I do not need your friendship."

"I'm sorry but if this gets to Nanny, I will tell her that you and Ken were kissing too."

Chebet was shocked at this attempt at blackmail.

"Sorry Grace, it's your choice," she remarked, before walking back to the hall.

She had to complete the narrative and present it to the music teacher the following day.

---•---

Chapter Twenty-five

A tense Chebet leant on the marble wall. She had been dreaming of this day and when it finally arrived, she could hardly sleep. Her school uniform was well pressed and her shoes brushed to a shine. She had almost no hair to comb. She wore the white pair of socks that Roselita bought her a month ago. Though she participated in the Luyia dance which had won in four previous festivals, her mind was on the narrative she was to present and which she knew left the audience in awe. The adjudicators she had met were positive of the narrative and commended her. She had won at the four levels and was now at the national level, where she represented Nairobi County in the week-long festival at the Kenyatta International Conference Centre which went by the short, easier name KICC. Their dance had also won. It was her first time at KICC. Roselita and the music teacher had accompanied her and kept on encouraging her.

She looked at the red carpet that covered the corridor. A young woman, dressed in khaki, was using a vacuum cleaner on the carpet. The pupils who lined the long corridor gave her the space to do the cleaning.

"Who will beat me among these pupils?" she studied the pupils, the majority of whom were quiet, probably putting final touches to their poems and narratives.

"Cheb, you have the opportunity to prove your ability to the world. You are gifted and have our support," she recalled Roselita's words. "If you win at the KICC, you will visit State House and perform for the President."

She smiled at the thought of visiting State House. It was so exciting a thought that for a moment she forgot what had befallen Rosemary. Her three children had been kidnapped. It had sent a chill down Chebet's spine to hear that Jeff may have been killed by the kidnappers after his parents took long to pay the ransom. The issue had gone national with the media giving it prominence. A debate was raging over irresponsible parenting, since the three children were kidnapped late at night after Roselita had left for the day. The guard was killed.

Rosemary had accused Roselita of involvement in the kidnap saying she was privy to the plan and had her arrested. She was, however, released two days later, for lack of evidence. Roselita did not go back to work for Rosemary after that.

"I do not have a job but don't worry… Make the best of the narrative. I have talked to Nanny and she has allowed me to accompany you," Roselita had told her the previous day.

"If I win, I will attribute the win to you, Auntie. I will pray for you to get another job."

"For now, it's the narrative that is important," Roselita had responded.

Chebet looked up at the ceiling as she recalled all these. The queue moved after every fifteen minutes. She was now approaching the entrance. Her heart raced, leaving her in a cold sweat.

"You are representing the whole of Nairobi. Do not let Nairobi down Chebet," her music teacher had told her, minutes before they were called to line up on the corridor.

"I wish I were representing my home county, Marigat," she had commented, making Roselita smile.

She moved a few steps forward and leant on the wall, recalling the gestures she was advised to employ, how she was to portray emotional changes during the presentation. The title of the narrative had been changed to "The Delegate."

It was her time to present. She matched boldly to the hall. She was directed to the centre and advised to wait.

The hall was full, with the judges and adjudicators at the front. Some were writing while others talked or looked at her. A few rows behind the judges sat Roselita and her music teacher. They were full of smiles and Chebet could not help but smile back. She held her hands behind her back nervously.

One of the judges rang the bell, signalling to her it was her turn. She breathed in deeply before starting.

"On the stage is Milcah Chebet from St Claire Primary School, representing Nairobi County. I have the pleasure to present a narration entitled 'The Delegate' that I wrote. Please sit back and enjoy." She bowed in respect;

Down in the valleys of Lucky You, a child is born.

A weak smile overwhelms the mother who is lying on her hard and bare bed.

She tries to lift the beautiful baby, but she cannot.

But, Oh God, the smile of the baby.

The smile of the innocent baby is wonderful.

But this baby

Ooh this baby.

She paused for effect.

Up in the highlands, another baby is born in a wonderful hospital. The mother smiles...

She continued with the narrative. They were quiet, all ears and eyes on her. The judges, too, stared at her; none wrote anything. They followed her emotions and gestures. They were enthralled.

When she finished with her narrative, the hall burst into a thunderous applause. Chebet looked at the audience with shyness but was also very pleased. According to her assessment, her expressions were real and not exaggerated. However, the girl who had preceded her was also good and had been received with about the same applause.

"Chebet, thank you for an impressive performance," one of the judges commented. "As you have heard from the composer herself, parents, be responsible and nurture that which you have been blessed with. Don't be too busy to the extent of transferring your parenting role to the housegirl. To the church, do not betray your role as the conscience, the moral compass and authority of society. To our beloved state, note that all children are equal. Our composer and presenter has told us so. She urged the children to make proper use of choices and to look ahead with hope and determination while shunning anything that may come between them and their growth. Let's clap again for this wonderful girl..." he led the audience in a round of applause.

"Thank you, Chebet, from Nairobi County."

Chebet walked off the stage. She could feel the eyes of the audience on her.

Roselita and the music teacher caught up with her before she got out through the main door.

"That was excellent! Congratulations my girl."

"Did I present it well? Do you think I will win? Will 'The Delegate' win?" she asked excitedly.

"No doubt about that," Roselita said as she buried Chebet in a warm embrace.

Chapter Twenty-six

Chebet sat on a log, a few metres away from the numerous enclosures that held cattle, goats and rabbits. Julius was busy feeding the rabbits, his task at the home – and one that he performed with utter seriousness and commitment. Since he did not have enough time on weekdays, he spent much of the weekend, specifically Saturday, looking after the rabbits. He did not have to wash his clothes – Chebet took care of that because she washed the clothes of the little children in the home. She had just finished the task and was at the sheds to spend some time with her brother as they waited for lunch. Dennis was in the field playing football with other boys.

"I miss our home. I miss my friends Ruto and Rotich. I miss all of them... Can we go home when we close school?"

"No, we cannot. You see, we are not employed nor have any income. When we start to work, after school, we shall leave the home," Chebet answered.

"Shall we go with Aunt Roselita? She is so good. I haven't seen her...."

"She travelled to her rural home after she lost her job. She is staying there for now."

"Will we ever see her again?" Julius asked with concern.

"Nanny said she will visit us tomorrow. When I grow up and get enough money, I will build her a house. She is one of the best people I have met in this world. Were it not for her, we wouldn't be here. I would still be working in the quarry and I would not have visited State House yesterday," Chebet said, a smile plastered on her face.

"Did you say that you shook hands with the president? Wow!" Julius exclaimed.

"The president shook my hand like this…" she demonstrated. "They had told me that I would see myself on the TV, but I did not see that yesterday. I took photos with him. The police refused us to take photos in the compound. It's so big and has so many beautiful buildings. I wish Aunt Roselita were there to accompany me. She was there when I won at the national music festival."

"Some people felt bad that you were going to State House. They said that we came just the other day and that we were being favoured and were given all the responsibilities," Julius told her.

"They have been here for a longer period of time. Why haven't they done the same? We beat them in the exams."

"Will they arrest Aunt Roselita again?" he asked.

"I do not think so. I heard from the radio that Jeff, Jean and Joy were released by the kidnappers. But Jeff was so traumatised, he was not talking."

"Why couldn't he talk?"

"I don't know. I think it's because of…" she paused when she noticed Sheila, her bedmate, approaching them.

"Nanny wants to dismiss Grace from the home. She caught her doing wrong things," Sheila told Chebet.

"It's no surprise. She has forgotten that she was picked from a dustbin by a Good Samaritan when she was a few weeks old."

"Yes. I heard that Grace had a phone, which someone bought her," Sheila continued.

"I would rather concentrate on my life and what will make my life better and that of Dennis and Julius," Chebet commented.

"What will you do when you grow up?" Sheila asked her, changing the subject.

"I want to be an advocate. I want to get justice for all the children. I would like to defend children against activities that degrade them. I want to impress upon them the value of being responsible and for children to understand their rights. Since the country has failed to stand up for the children, I want to come in and assist. Many children are suffering; I will be their ambassador and will represent them when it comes to dealing with the state, church and parents," Chebet said passionately.

"Wow! That's great," Sheila responded. "How do you start that?"

"I have already started, Sheila. My narrative was all about that. Can I perform it for you?"

Chebet started but was interrupted by her brother who came running.

"What's wrong, Dennis?" Julius asked as he closed the door of one of the sheds.

"Chebet, you are wanted at the office."

"What?"

"Yes."

"I guess it's about Grace," Sheila commented.

As she approached the office, shaken and unsure of what awaited her, Chebet saw Nanny beside a metallic blue Toyota Prado.

"Sorry, but if any of these gets to Nanny, I will tell her that you and Ken were kissing too." Chebet recalled Grace's words with fear. She had not told Nanny anything; maybe Grace thought she did.

"What if Grace included me in the case?" her heart beat faster. "What if I am chased away from the home?"

She did not wish to leave the home but knew Nanny could easily order her out. She was a good person. However, when annoyed, she could do anything. She had chased away two girls and one boy for misbehaving. The three were ferried back to their relatives in a rented car. She escorted them to ensure they were returned to their relatives. Chebet would not want such a thing to happen. She thought of what she would say, if indeed Grace had falsely told on her.

Julius and Dennis followed her to the office.

Chapter Twenty-seven

Chebet followed Nanny to her simple office. Her heartbeat accelerated, especially after she saw Grace standing behind the Prado, her eyes wet with tears. Bobby stood a few metres away from Grace. He, too, looked very worried. He looked away when their eyes met.

She knocked respectfully at the door, praying that Nanny would not notice her discomfort.

"Please come in Chebet," Nanny responded after she settled on her leather seat. There were two women who sat facing each other across the table. She studied them as she entered the office and stood beside the table, almost leaning on the file cabinet.

"Greet our guests, Chebet," Nanny said, a smile spread on her face.

"Were these the relatives of Grace?" Chebet wondered as she shook hands with each of them. Their palms were soft. One of the women had long and painted nails. Her dress barely reached the knees, leaving her thighs exposed. The other woman was in a full dress.

"If these were the relatives of Grace, then she wouldn't be here. The home is basically for orphans," she concluded.

"These are your guests Chebet," Nanny said.

Chebet studied them innocently.

"I'm Deborah Davis," the lady with the mini-skirt introduced herself, speaking with an accent that placed her anywhere but Kenya.

"This is Terry-Anne Aluoch," she pointed at her colleague who held a white envelope in her left hand. She smiled at Chebet.

"We have come because of your performance at State House. The Canadian High Commissioner was impressed by your determination and intellect."

Chebet wanted to say thank you but there was no chance to do that.

"We followed up and learnt that your story is a unique one. It would be interesting to hear it from you. Anyway, we have delivered the message from the High Commissioner..." She took the white envelope from her colleague and gave it to Chebet.

"Kindly read the message and let us know what you think," Deborah smiled. Chebet glanced at Nanny as if to seek permission.

"Do not fear. Open the letter," Nanny urged her.

Chebet removed a letter from the envelope and unfolded it, her hands shaking with anticipation.

"Nomination as a Children's Delegate to the United Nations," was the heading of the letter. She got confused as she did not understand what the message meant. She read on:

"We are pleased to nominate you as a Delegate to the forthcoming United Nations Children's Conference to represent Africa's children. The conference will be held in Geneva, Switzerland, from the 16th to the 20th November, 2012.

We are also inviting either a parent or a guardian to accompany you to the conference.

The Canadian High Commission will pay for all travel and accommodation expenses for you and your parent or guardian."

Chebet did not finish reading the letter. Tears of joy and incredulity streamed down her cheeks. She would be inside an aeroplane in the next six weeks.

"It's true Chebet. You are a living story to children all over the world. We would like you to represent African children at the conference. The conference will culminate in the celebration of the Universal Children's Day. You will be one of the many representatives of various continents," Deborah commented.

"As we informed you, it was a process. Chebet was investigated after her name was submitted to the committee that was looking for the best child to represent Africa. This started immediately after she won at the National Music Festival at KICC. That's where her potential was identified and what followed was validation of her story and getting to know more of her."

"We did not know anything was going on," Nanny commented.

"We did not want anyone to know; otherwise facts could have been distorted."

"Anyway who will accompany you my dear? You will need someone to accompany you as you travel to Geneva," Deborah told her.

Chebet was still in tears but of joy.

"I have Roselita. She is like a mother to me…" she looked at Nanny and noticed some sadness on her face. "I will go with Roselita. She is out of a job. I am happy to do something for her."

"The Commission was right," Terry commented. "You have the best of hearts, girl."

Chebet smiled.

She studied the letter once more and felt like jumping up and down in excitement.

"I am a United Nations Delegate for Children," she smiled some more.

"You will not regret choosing me," she said, holding the letter to her chest. "I promise to be the best delegate for the children of Africa."

She longed for the meeting to end for her to share the news with her brothers. She could not wait for tomorrow to break the news to Roselita.

Chapter Twenty-eight

Chebet looked at herself in the mirror. The pink blouse made her adorable. Her hair was short and neat. The thought that her short hair made her look like a boy did not bother her at all. She turned and looked at herself and a broad smile beamed across her face. She glanced at the wristwatch Father Joachim had bought her and realised that time was moving at a snail's pace. They were supposed to leave Nairobi aboard a Kenya Airways aeroplane at 8 PM, six hours away. She had just talked to the children at the home promising to represent them well. The home, including the owner, bought her a dress, a pair of shoes and a handbag. St Claire, through the sister in charge, bought several jackets, while the church gave her an expensive travelling bag.

Chebet had become an instant celebrity with gifts and friends flowing in. She visited several high profile offices, including the Canadian High Commissioner's, which was paying for Chebet and Roselita's travel. Roselita was initially reluctant to accompany Chebet. The appointment gave Chebet an opportunity to see Roselita's children who came accompanied by their father to see her off. Roselita was distressed by that and hardly talked to her ex-husband who strolled in the compound, deep in thought.

Chebet walked out of the room and met her two brothers standing by the dining hall.

"The Delegate! The Delegate!" children at the home called out as she passed. Dennis moved towards her, sucking on his thumb. A vehicle from the Canadian High Commission, which would carry them to the airport, was parked at the assembly ground.

Chebet did not know how to carry herself especially now that all eyes were on her.

"What will you bring us, Cheb?" Dennis asked innocently, still sucking on his thumb.

"You and Julius will forever remain top on my priorities."

"We will miss you, Cheb."

"I know, I will miss you too. I came to Nairobi because I wanted to help you and ensure that you complete school. I had vowed to quit school for the sake of your future. I will never forget you, okay, Julius? I will bring you gifts."

"I want to be like you, Cheb. Aunt Roselita told me that we shall go to the airport to see you fly off," Dennis commented, ignoring the other children who were standing by Chebet. "Are you worried?"

"No, I have Aunt Roselita, but I'm anxious."

Roselita emerged from the hall in a black suit. Her ex-husband watched them from a distance. He was standing beside his white BMW, his children by his side.

"Chebet, the High Commissioner has called Nanny. She has said we leave early. We should start our journey now…" she said softly. Nanny was approaching them, a handbag in her hands. She was to drive Julius and Dennis to the airport. Chebet noticed some sadness in Roselita.

"Are you well, Auntie?"

"I have just been informed that Jeff died last night."

"What?"

"Yes, he succumbed to the trauma."

"Oh, my God."

Just then Nanny reached them to announce it was time to leave. Chebet waved at the children but did not realise that she had started to shed tears. She did not know why she was crying.

"Please speak to us, Cheb!" one of the boys at the home shouted.

"Okay," she paused, "I'm proud to be a member of this home. What is happening to me is a sign that everything is possible. It does not matter where you come from or who your parents are; what matters is your determination and discipline in pursuing your goals." She remembered Jeff. "We may be victims of fate but we can choose how to live our lives. Whether we lack in very essential human needs, always remember that we can model our lives and live a very successful life. This is my message to you. Wherever I am going, I will have you in my heart. You are all wonderful people. Before I leave, I request that you pray for the soul of someone that I know who died recently. He is called Jeff. Please pray for his soul. Thank you."

She removed a handkerchief from the handbag and wiped away her tears. The children clapped continuously, following her to the Canadian High Commission vehicle. She waved at them, before they drove off.

"This is happening because of you, Auntie. Thank you so much," she told Roselita.

"No. As you said, it was all your choice. I'm the one to thank you. Thank you so much Madam Delegate," Roselita tapped her shoulders. Chebet remained quiet for a while.

"However, it is unfortunate that we shall not attend Jeff's burial," she remarked.

Chebet looked at the waving crowd and for a moment forgot about Jeff. She waved at her teachers who stood by the gate of the school.

They waved back excitedly. She then leant back on the seat and closed her eyes.

"You wi-ll quit sch-ool and get ma-rri-ed. Talk to yo-ur uncle Nor-be-rt. He wi-ll org-an-i-se for that and your initi-a-tion. Take ca-re of…" she recalled her mother's advice as she lay dying. "Mum, I know you and Father are very happy wherever you are," she thought quietly. "I am now a delegate."

She wondered how her life was going to change now that she was a delegate.

"Will I remain in the same school? What if I don't come back here? What about my brothers? How will the meeting in Switzerland be? No, time will tell," she told herself. "That will be another story, which I will tell when I come back. Maybe I will call it Kenya, here I come."

She looked out through the window at an aeroplane that was flying past. In the next few hours, she, too, would be in the sky flying. She smiled broadly. Roselita was looking at her admiringly; she, too, smiled when their eyes met.

"The fact that you are meeting bad people does not mean that there are no good people," she thought proudly.

She leant on the seat and closed her eyes.

"I will have to write about my story," she resolved quietly.

Printed in the United States
By Bookmasters